Lost in
Frenetic Catatonia

Lost in
Frenetic Catatonia

by
Winston Roberts

2019

First Printing: 2019

ISBN: 9781687698865

Dedication

For Lillian and William.

For John and Alyssa.

For Jackie.

For Goodness sake.

Contents

The Reluctant Husband..1

Atlantis..9

Electronic Prison 17

First date 24

The Writer's Recursion 29

Cultural Differences 33

Technological Barriers 46

The Vacation..60

The Gargoyle 85

Symphonic Dissonance 95

Family Reunion..107

Miss Prog Nosis 120

The Forty Percent Genius..126

The Whispers..133

A Birthday Surprise..137

The Reluctant Husband

The car door just wouldn't open. 'Just Perfect!', she whispered under her breath. She looked up into a crystal blue sky and invoked any gods, that there be, to help her get through this day without a homicide. There was only so much a woman could take. There was only so much energy in the tank to deal with any bullsh*t. She had had it, as it were.

Carmella Franks, or Carmella Lawson as she was now known, had just left the lawyers offices where she signed the divorce agreement. Why in the whole wide world she had ever taken up with that no good, lazy ass, selfish son of a living and breathing mixed breed mangy lady dog was way beyond her right now. She was so livid her eyes were bulging in her head. The summer heat did nothing to help the situation. She could just scream.

And so, she did. Loud and long. The other folks in the parking lot turned to see what was going on. They got a good look at a crazy woman letting off some steam. One lady turned to her friend and remarked, "Probably just got a divorce." Her friend laughed. They had known the pain very well.

Carmella swung her purse at the door. The door cracked open.

Carmella had given her husband, Joey, the best years of her life and what she had for it was a measly check for $3543. That was the sum total of their wealth in over 18 years of marriage. It seemed such a waste of time. She had given the marriage everything she had but she just couldn't make it work. Or make HIM work, for that matter. Joey was a loathsome down right dog of a man to her now. If she never ever in her blessed cage free life ever saw him again, she would count herself as the happiest of women. In fact, if she never ever saw another man at all, she would consider her fate to have been one of complete and utter victory.

The car door dilemma solved; Carmella drove home to her little farmhouse near Hudson's creek. She stopped at the liquor store for a couple of bottles of red, and heck why not a couple more of white. She had a notion she might just drink up the entire $3543 but decided that some of it might come in handy later.

Her pig, Dalton, met her at the door. Carmella loved Dalton. He was the only constant in her life. He gave her unconditional love and asked for nothing in return except table scraps and maybe the occasional musk melon. Maybe some corn with that and a cabbage or two. Heck if there was any expired bread that would be nice as well. Dalton loved to eat, as most pigs do, I guess.

Carmella opened the first bottle and poured a 24-ounce big gulp plastic cup full. She moseyed off to the front porch and sat in her favorite chair. The sun was setting over the hill beyond her house. She sat and fumed.

She went back to the kitchen to refill her cup and brought another bottle back with her to prevent her stewing from being interrupted by trips to the kitchen. She fumed and sat and drank. And fumed. When she was done, she did it all over again. And then a thought entered her alcohol addled brain. It was an idea of genius. An idea so beautiful she marveled that no one had ever had the idea before. It seemed perfect in its symmetry. The idea had merit. She began to design a plan.

She, being through with all men for all time, decided that what she had wanted in the first place was a companion. She wanted someone to share her life with, someone to be there in her ups and downs. Someone to be a soul mate. Someone to love and to be loved by that someone.

She didn't necessarily need a physical relationship. She had a mechanical device in her bedroom side table that was very efficient in that area. No, what she needed was more of a spiritual nature. If not spiritual, then emotional/psychological. It was then, from this, that the idea sprouted.

Who was her best friend? Who had always been there for her? Who would never leave her? The answer was obvious. It was Dalton all along! Dalton was her friend. He loved her like no mere man could. Dalton would be her soulmate. Dalton would be her husband!

The next day, after some serious hangover therapies, Carmella got to work. She brought out some of Joey's old clothes he had left and dragged her sewing machine out from under the coffee table in the living room. She piled the stuff up high on the dining room table and began her work.

Dalton would need to look stylish. She had always wanted a stylish husband. A bon vivant. A lady's man, that she had corralled. A Dalton already had the taste for good food, he just needed the clothes to match.

She would make him a set of clothes for every occasion. He needed lounging wear and evening wear. He needed work clothes (he would have to work, every husband needed a job), he needed pajamas. She decided to go semi-formal on the street clothes. She wanted Dalton to look trendy, not stuffy. A jeans jacket and a scarf would do nicely for those trips to the coffee shop.

Working well into the night, Carmella finally stood to admire her work. The clothes looked perfect. Now for Dalton to try them on.

Carmella used the old horse trough outside for cleaning things like her hands after gardening. Or sometimes she had some jeans that were especially muddy, and she would give them a rinse out there before throwing them in the laundry inside the house. Today Dalton would use the trough. Carmella wanted him clean if he was going to live in the house.

Now Dalton was unimpressed with clean things. His greatest pleasures came from rolling in mud and rooting up the ground looking for edibles. Dalton knew that Carmella wanted him to get in the trough, but he really didn't see the point.

Carmella was insistent, though. She grabbed poor Dalton by the front legs and threw them over the rim of the trough. Having the front legs situated, she grabbed his hind quarters and levered the squirming hog into the trough. The clean water in the trough turned a dark brown almost immediately. Carmella picked up a scrub brush and vigorously scoured her poor new husband from snout to tail.

The wrestling match in the trough now complete, Carmella wrapped her prize in a beach towel and brought him into the house. Dalton resisted the going inside part. He had spent his life outside, roaming where he wanted inside the fenced area. The house seemed rather closed in and it triggered his porcine claustrophobia.

The happy couple made the journey, however, with Carmella carrying Dalton over the threshold. The next task was the clothes part. Dalton eyed the pile of clothes on the dining room table. Nothing good could come from that, he estimated. Dalton made a run for the kitchen. Carmella would prevent his escape by a strategic plopping of a dining table chair in the path to freedom.

The wrestling continued. Pig and woman were matched in an epic struggle for clothing dominance. The pig squealed his displeasure as the lady remonstrated him for behaving so badly. Every marriage had its fights, and this was their second one already in one day. In time the woman won, as is usually the case, and Dalton stood on all fours clothed in skinny jeans and a form fitting top made of silk. The ensemble was completed with a fedora and red pattern bandana.

The struggle to get even this outfit on Dalton left Carmella satisfied that maybe he could sleep in it tonight. Just this once. She was dying to see him in the pajamas she had made. They were flannel cut in a Ralph Lauren Soho type fit. Dalton would look quite the connoisseur of haute couture in those.

The days went by and Dalton and Carmella lived in harmony in their little honeymoon cabin in the woods. Well it was like on a farmette and near some trees, but let's just go with the woods thing. In either case, Carmella felt a joy that had been missing in her life. She had the companion she always wanted. She was happy.

Dalton, on the other hand … er … hoof, wasn't as happy. The woman kept dressing him up in these restrictive pieces of cloth. He was used to running free and untethered, as it were, and the clothing thing, he really did not get. He was constantly on the lookout for a way to break free of his jailer, but Carmella was ever vigilant at keeping the doors closed.

But not the windows.

One hot and humid night, Carmella opened all the downstairs windows to try and get a cross breeze going. The air in the house was stale and stifling. Dalton saw his chance. Using his prodigious snout, Dalton edged a coffee table next to the front window that led out to the front porch. When he had it properly positioned, he jumped on the coffee table, then out of the window and down on the porch. The entire operation took seconds. Before he could tell if Carmella had heard, he was off and running down the dirt road that connected the farm to the outside world. He did not stop until miles down the road at the Harper farm.

Carmella, having prepared for bed, had not noticed her darling husband's escape from their love nest domicile. She looked all around the house for the pig but could not find a clue. It was then she saw the coffee table. It had little pig like prints on it.

Carmella started feeling that old rage welling up inside her. She was feeling like she felt when she divorced that good for nothin' Joey. Could she have been abandoned by two men in the same year? The thought made her head ache and her hands tremble. She vowed this would not go unpunished.

Carmella was up early the next day with a dog collar and leash, hunting for Dalton. She checked each bush and fence line from her house to the Harper farm. When she reached the Harper compound, she was met by Bob Harper.

"You lookin' for Dalton?" Bob spit some chewing tobacco out of his mouth and put his thumbs inside the straps of his overalls.

"You seen him?" Carmella's face was fixed in a stone cold stare of absolute focus and resolution.

"Come with me."

Bob led Carmella down to the pig sty and there neck deep in mud was her Dalton, with two of Bob Harpers sows. The betrayal was too much for poor Carmella. Gritting her teeth, she barked at Bob.

"Help me get him out."

↔

The next day, Carmella answered her front door. It was her girlfriend, Hilary. Carmella invited her in and escorted her to the kitchen. The smell of frying meat and potatoes wafted through the air.

"Hungry?"

"Sure!" Hilary took a seat at the kitchen table. "But what I really came for was to meet your new guy? Is this Dalton dude around?"

"Oh, he's around." Carmella got two plates down from the cabinet. She placed one in front of Hilary.

"One chop or two?"

"Two please." Hilary salivated at the feast to come. "How is your new beau then? Is he cute?"

"I ended it with him, the cheatin' scum." Carmella placed two chops on Hilary's plate. "He was a good provider, though. He could literally bring home the bacon."

The women ate in silence. Carmella was the first to talk.

"Men are such pigs!"

Atlantis

He adjusted the aluminum foil collar around his neck. The collar needed to fit around his entire neck if he was to keep the government from reading his thoughts. He had taken to the streets years before to avoid them. He stayed on constant watch for them, the men in the blue uniforms. He had had plenty of their prisons with all those crazy people they put around him to put him off his game. If he stayed vigilant, he could avoid that fate.

The cardboard box that had been his blanket for the night was soaked through. The rain had been heavy. He had managed to keep relatively dry, however. He threw the box to the side and made his way down the alley into the street beyond.

The donut shop was open and full of commuters getting their caffeine and sugar fixes. He plopped himself down on the sidewalk. Maybe one of them would offer him some sustenance. Most days they would. He looked at his reflection in the mirror. The man there was unrecognizable. He had long matted hair and a long scraggly beard. His coat was ragged and looked like he had slept in it. He had slept in it. Many nights.

A police car approached. The men in blue were inside. He decided to take a walk. Nothing good ever came of an encounter with the men in blue. He walked down the street to the docks by the river. He made this journey every day, hoping that one day the boat would be there. The boat that would take him away. Take him away to Atlantis. He would be happy in Atlantis. They could turn down the noises in his head. They could take away the pains.

He sat with his back to the wall of one of the warehouses where he could get a panoramic view of the river. The boats were already about their daily tasks. He searched for his boat; it would have an angel at the helm. None were evident today. He would keep watch, just in case.

He pulled the stone out of his pocket. It was a small round smooth stone, blue and black. The boy had given it to him. He couldn't remember the boy. Every time he tried to remember he developed a blinding pain in his head. His vision was replaced by a piercing light filling the entire field of his view. The back of his head felt like a knife had been inserted and twisted. He tried not to think about the boy. It was better that way.

The blue men had probably left the donut shop by now, so he decided to return there. He wanted to check on the ringleader. The big cheese. The one who controlled everything. The big boss would be leaving his bar soon, the 'Tipsy Doodle'. The boss would call his car to come pick him up. The boss' goons would accompany him. The boss was no good. The boss was what was wrong with it all.

The boss could call the blue men. The blue men knew the boss and did his bidding. The boss knew the government.

The boss was in charge of the government. He had to keep good tabs on the boss. The boss could put him back in the prison. They could put him in the prison. They could read his thoughts there.

He resumed his position by the donut shop. It shouldn't be long now. The boss liked to keep a tight schedule. A goon with a ponytail and sweater vest appeared. The car would be next.

The car pulled around the building and parked in its usual place in front of the bar's front door. The goon opened the back door of the black sedan and waited. He wouldn't wait long.

The boss exited his establishment of liquor and entertainment and surveyed the street. A coat of some kind of wild exotic animal adorned the shoulders of the big guy. He was big. Tall and yet fat. The boss wore his alligator shoes today. He loved those shoes. They were his favorites.

The boss looked to his left and to his right. The street looked quiet enough. The boss had many enemies. His appraisal of the scene satisfied him that he was in no immediate danger. The boss walked to the car and sat down in the back seat. The goon closed the door and entered the passenger seat in the front. The car sped away.

He decided to go to the park to sleep a bit. The boss wouldn't be back until nightfall. He could while away the day soaking up the sun and listening to the birds. He stopped by a man purveying pretzels. He loved the smell. The roastey salty chewy smell of the fresh pretzels. He sat behind the man's cart.

It wasn't long and a young man bought a pretzel. He covered the treat with mustard, just the way that he had liked them when he was buying them. The young man turned to walk away and bumped into a pedestrian walking by. The bump jostled the pretzel from the man's grasp and the bready snack fell to the ground. The young man sighed and picked up the pretzel and threw it in the trash.

Now, an uneaten pretzel in the trash can was an invitation for him. He had eaten a lot worse in his struggle to stay clear of the government. He ambled to the can and picked the pretzel from atop a pile of other trash. He took a bite. It was still warm. Delicious.

His belly filled, he found his favorite tree and settled down for a midday nap. He pulled his coat tight around his chin to keep in the warmth. He made sure his aluminum foil collar was correctly positioned. In minutes he was far away in a dream.

He languished on a pristine lawn of freshly mown grass. The sun baked his aging body. A bird with blue feathers and a long black beak came and rested on his chest. The bird had something in its bill. He took the piece of paper from its beak and read.

'It is time. You know what to do.'

He looked at the bird. "What does it mean?"

The bird responded. "It is time." The bird flew away.

The bird hadn't made much sense. What time? Also, he did not know what to do. He rose from his resting place in the grass and followed the bird as it flew. The bird darted here then there. Suddenly, as suddenly as the bird had arrived, it was gone. He was left at the edge of a forest. The whole world was silent. The silence hurt his ears. They were used to constant noise.

A lady emerged from the forest. She was clothed in white and radiated a gossamer glow. He recognized the lady. She was the one. The one from Atlantis. She was to take him home there.

"Have you come for me?" He reached out his hand to touch her.

"Not yet my dear one." She touched his hand with hers. "You have one thing left to do."

"One thing?"

"Yes." She bade him sit, then she sat in front of him. "Look in your pocket."

He reached deep in his pocket and pulled the stone out. The stone the boy had given him. "This?"

"Yes. That's it."

She put her hands together in a meditative pose and bowed her head. He, not knowing what to do, assumed the same posture. In time they rose. He before, not knowing, now he did know.

"I understand." He reached to touch her once more, but she had already started her return to the forest.

With the coming of night, it had started to rain, and the rain woke him from his slumber. He rubbed the water from his eyes and started his journey. He had a task to perform. It would be his last. She would take him after, he was assured.

He weaved in and out of the pedestrian traffic. The mobs of workers leaving for the day made the going slow. He knew every short cut in the city, every alleyway. He would not be late for his assignment. He would make it on time no matter the obstacle.

In time, he reached the donut shop. The bar across the street was filling with patrons. Some for an afterwork drink, some for a couple of afterwork drinks. How many times had he beheld this scene? How many times had he sat and watched as the boss returned from his daily routine? But tonight, would be different.

He crossed the street putting his hand over his eyes to prevent the rain from blurring his vision. He walked to the spot. It was the spot where he had seen the boss emerge from his car a thousand times. He knew the spot well.

He put his hand into his pocket and retrieved the stone. The one the boy had given him. His boy. His son. He put the stone on the pavement, just before the curb. This is where the boss put his foot when exiting the car. The boss. The one that had killed his son.

All that was left now was to wait. He crossed back over to the alleyway beside the donut shop. He didn't mind the rain now. He didn't mind getting soaked to the bone. This was his last task. He would be leaving soon.

The boss' car returned right on time. The goon in the passenger seat, the guy with the ponytail and sweater vest, jumped out of the car and pulled an umbrella open. He stepped to the back door and opened it for the boss. The boss stepped out.

He looked on in anxious anticipation. The boss had taken the bait. What would happen next was out of his hands. She had assured him of his success in the operation. She had assuaged any doubt. He was fully confident of what should transpire next.

The boss reached out to take the umbrella when the rock underneath his foot, the smooth round rock, the one the boy had given the man across the street at the donut shop, the boy the boss had killed, rolled under the sole of the expensive alligator shoes. The shoes the boss loved.

The rolling of the stone caused the boss to lose his balance. Losing his balance, the boss toppled. The boss fell. The boss hit the ground, but not before his head landed on the solid concrete curb beside the pavement. The boss hit his head, and the boss' head exploded, spewing blood and part of his brain onto the ever-wetter asphalt.

He looked on, not with glee, but with sadness. The boss had paid for the crime, but it had not healed the pain he felt. The blinding headache returned. He knelt under its grip. He held his hands to the sides of his head to prevent the headache from exploding his own head.

He stumbled toward the river, toward the dock. He found his place against the wall of the warehouse. The wall proved a workable shelter from the rain. He looked up and down the river for the boat. She had promised she would be there.

The pain in his head started to wane. The embolism in his brain had burst. He felt the energy draining from his body. He was dying, he knew it. He relaxed his body in a final surrender to the pain. A surrender to the grief. To the rage. Slowly his vision started to dim. He looked one last time to the river.

There, at the helm of the boat, was the lady in white with the gossamer radiance. She would take him to Atlantis.

Electronic Prison

The screen was black. It had been black for some time now. He wondered when it was going to come back. He would sit and be patient. The screen had gone dark before but had eventually relit. The screen would display images again, he just knew it. The screen wouldn't let him down. Not now. Not after all they had been through.

Harvey sat in his living room with the curtains drawn. The recliner he enjoyed was cocked in the upright position. It was the position he used for his gaming. He had been embroiled in an epic battle for possession of the castle and the rescue of the princess when his monitor had gone dark. Harvey was a little confused. He really didn't know what to do.

Harvey called for his domestic mechanical. "Hey James! Come in here will ya'?" He had named the device James after a favorite character from the movies.

James wheeled into the living room. "Yes sir. How may I be of service." Harvey had put James in British butler mode. He enjoyed the illusion of Victorian luxury.

"The screen's black." Harvey pointed to the giant display wall where his images used to be constantly displayed.

"I see." James computed a set of possible responses and scenarios. "I will check the system sir. Just one moment." James wheeled away.

Harvey pulled back the lever on his recliner to lay him flat. Secretly, he welcomed the respite from the screen. He could relax his eyes for a minute. Harvey closed his eyes and began to slip into sleep.

Harvey was woken from his slumber by a crashing sound coming from the kitchen area. He pushed the lever on the recliner and bolted up right. Harvey jogged to the kitchen.

There on the limestone encrusted vinyl lay James. He had fallen over on his side. His wheels, which were James' only source of propulsion, spun in clean kitchen air. James' vision eye was dark. James was not moving. James looked as dead as the screen in the living room.

This was a situation in which Harvey had never been challenged. He had no screen. He had no James. What he did have was hunger, but James was always responsible for that. Harvey would just have to try and do it himself. He would worry about the screen later.

Harvey perused the kitchen. The cabinet doors of the space were smooth with no visible hardware for human hands to manipulate the doors. Harvey tried to open one of them, but it wouldn't give to the force his hands gave as they swept over the surface of the door.

Harvey looked underneath the door. It had a small eyehole there, presumably for some tool James possessed.

Harvey looked to James' articulating appendages. There were an array of tools and grips on his hands. Harvey tried to pull one of the metal implements from James' hand, but the tool was firmly ensconced there. It would not move.

Harvey looked around. There was nothing available for exploration of the eyehole. Harvey searched the house. He tried the bedroom and closets. He opened drawers. Nothing looked useable. Then, in the bathroom, he found it. His toothbrush.

Bringing the tooth cleaning device back to the kitchen, Harvey set to opening one of the cabinets yet again. The handle of the toothbrush was close to the size needed but it was a bit too wide. Harvey would have to cut it down. He looked for a knife. They were in the cabinets. Harvey threw his toothbrush to the ground in disgust.

Harvey reached deep into the pockets of his shirt. It was the resting place for his smart pad. The smart pad would save him. He'd order from the Flaming Dragon, his favorite Thai restaurant. They delivered. Zippidee Dooda and he had his pad at his fingertips.

The pad failed to respond to his touch. He tried the buttons on the side the tablet. No go. He pressed his fingers onto the scan button in an attempt to login with his fingerprints, but that too proved fruitless. His smart pad met his toothbrush on the kitchen floor.

His home was useless to him now. He would have to drive to civilized electronically activated society. He headed for the garage.

The electric car, that was Harvey's pride and some of his joy, stood prominent in the middle of the garage, its electric charging cord umbilical tethered between the car and the charging station on the wall. Harvey unplugged the car and jumped into the driver's seat. He called the car to action.

"Power on."

Harvey sat. And waited. The large display on the dashboard was as dark as his screen inside. Harvey tried again.

"I said, POWER ON!"

Using a louder volume did nothing to coax the car to life. Harvey stared at the screen. In time a small icon appeared on the display. It was the outline of a battery done in red color. Red was the color of empty in this model. Under the battery icon were the words.

"Low battery."

Harvey pounded his fist on top of the dashboard. "Just work dammit!"

The battery icon slowly faded away. The display went black.

Harvey went back inside. He had no idea what to do now. Everything he depended on in life had failed. He returned to the comfort of his recliner. He felt safe there. He felt … well … loved there.

Harvey clicked the recliner into the lay down mode. He stared at the ceiling of the living room, perhaps for the first time. The ceiling had been finished with a texturing of sorts. Harvey imagined all kinds of patterns emerging from the seemingly random pattern in the texture. He saw a malformed donkey here. There was a rabbit there with three ears.

The thing that started to bother him, the thing that was worrying, was the silence. It was so quiet. The house was never this quiet. There was always the sound of whirring cooling fans for the electronics or the heating and cooling systems.

But it wasn't just silent. There were sounds. Every now and then there would be a creak or crackle as the house groaned in the wind outside.

His imagination started to run amok at the small little sounds. Harvey became preoccupied with the sounds. His mind started to interpret each bump and pop. Was there an intruder? A murderer lurking about? Perhaps the sounds were otherworldly. Perhaps there was a spirit at work. Was the spirit malevolent? Was he in danger of losing his life? His very soul?

Harvey curled his body in a fetal position. He would ride out this black screen time of his life. All would be well if he just waited. If he just believed.

Detective Hanson opened the front door of the house. He was met immediately with the repugnant stink of death.

The neighbors were right. Something had happened to Harvey.

The Detective ordered the patrolmen to open the windows, to give them a chance to investigate, the smell was that pervasive. In time, Detective Hanson braved the fetid cloud of decomposition and investigated the property for any and all corpses.

Hanson found Harvey tightly curled in a ball lying on his recliner. He didn't need to go further. He would call the coroner for the autopsy. There were no signs of a struggle. Suicide seemed the best explanation at the moment.

Night had fallen and so the detective reached for a light switch to illuminate the room. The switch failed to light the lamps in the ceiling. He tried the switches in the kitchen. No luck there. Detective Hanson visited the garage. He knew this neighborhood put the breaker cabinet there.

Hanson opened the door of the breaker panel. A quick inspection revealed that the main power fuse had been tripped. 'Power surge'. Hanson diagnosed the trouble. The detective clicked the main fuse back to its working position.

The lights in the garage fired. The whirring of electrical motors starting to wind up filled the house. The detective revisited the living room. It was fully lit, and the display wall was already filling with icons and various windows displaying various content.

A voice called out from the kitchen. "May I have some assistance, please?"

The detective entered the kitchen to find a robotic domestic device lying on the floor. He picked it up and righted the device.

"Thank you, sir." James motored to the living room to see if Harvey needed anything.

First Date

The mall was abustle with families running, shopping and eating. Little children were crying. They understood not why their parents had brought them to this venue of total mayhem. All they wanted was a rest and a box of juice. They enjoyed their comforts. No, the mall was not for them.

Seats were hard to find. They did that so you did more shopping than sitting. Across the center of the mall he spotted and empty bench. He started for it. He needed to reserve it. He just about made it, too, when an old couple plopped down on it right in front of him.

The day before, Jason had passed a note to Kiki Ledbetter in class asking her if she wanted to meet at the mall today.

'Do you want to meet me at the mall on Saturday?

__ Yes

__ No

If Yes:

__ at 1:00

__ at 2:00 '

To his delight, Kiki had checked he 'Yes' box on the note and handed it back to him. She also had opted for the earlier time, 1:00. Jason was aquiver. Kiki was one of the popular girls in school. He loved the way she always had her hair done up with a ribbon. She was pretty and smart and everything for which a twelve-year-old boy was looking.

Jason walked the circumference of the atrium. The escalators droned their stairways up and down. People were laughing. A mother was scolding an ornery child. And then he spotted it. A completely empty bench recently vacated by a family of four. He dove for the bench before some other old people grabbed it.

Jason waited. He placed his jacket on the bench beside him to warn any usurpers that this was his territory. None need apply for seating there. That space was reserved for the lovely Kiki.

Jason kept going over in his mind how he was to play the date. He would have to be witty and charming if he was to have any chance with Kiki. Kiki was the kind of girl who could choose who she wanted as her beau and Jason wanted that to be him.

Jason's palms were sweaty. His hands shook with the rapidity of advanced Parkinson's. He detected a sudden dryness in his mouth, but he would not, nay, could not leave his post on the bench lest someone snatch it up. Everything had to be perfect. He would have to power through the dryness.

His shirt was beginning to exhibit a bit of moisture around the underarm area. He dropped his nose down for an investigative sniff. The area seemed somewhat perfumed if a bit wet. Jason decided it would pass. He cursed himself for not having applied a second layer of deodorant.

A group of young girls entered the mall's atrium. Kiki was right in the middle of the group. Jason dared not approach the girls as, again, he might give up the bench. He decided to wave to see if Kiki could be brought closer by his signaling.

Kiki's eyes met his and she smiled at his wave. She said something to her friends and then walked his way. Jason started to freak at this. It had all been theoretical until now. Her approach made it real.

"Hi." Jason moved his jacket for her to sit.

"Hi." Kiki brushed her long blond brown hair over her shoulder.

Jason froze. He had rehearsed so many lines of dialogue for this meeting that he was having trouble selecting the one that was appropriate for a just sitting down phase. He racked his brain, and nothing came to the fore. Finally, he just blurted what was available between brain and tongue.

"I ... I ... I won third prize." Jason cursed himself for such egoistic nonsense.

Kiki looked at Jason, first, not sure what exactly he meant, and second, not sure exactly what he had won. "Oh."

Jason felt completed defeated. He would have to make the next one count. He needed to get back in her good graces, if only to reassure her of his sanity.

"Did you know …" Jason said this at the exact same time that Kiki said, "How did you …"

The pair smiled a nervous smile and looked the other way. Jason was first to recover.

"Please, you first." Jason regained a bit of self-respect in this. He had used the word, 'please', and he now put the onus of conversation on her.

"It's just that I was wondering what you won for?"

Jason had not anticipated this. He had won third place for his diorama of the Battle of Yorktown for his mother's DAR group. It was not the coolest contest or prize. Actually, there just four entries and little David Walkins was never in the running as his diorama had been built out of toilet paper and chewing gum.

"Oh, nothing." Jason thought this the best answer. Too much information at this point would only make him look bad.

Kiki sat quietly. She was losing interest, he could tell. It was time to bring out the big guns. Jason reached in his pocket and produced a hand full of lemon drop candies. Some had some lint on them. He tried to brush the lint off with his thumb as he offered them to Kiki.

"Oh, thank you." Kiki selected one of the most lint free ones.

Jason took one himself and together they sat on the bench enjoying their candies. In silence.

After a while, Kiki broke the silence. "Well, I gotta go."

Jason jumped to his feet. "Ok."

Kiki flipped her long blond brown hair to the other shoulder. "See you in school?"

"Yeah."

Kiki leaned over and kissed Jason on the cheek. She then turned and left, searching out her girlfriends.

Jason felt his face turning a deep shade of red. His heart rate was through the roof. He felt as if his body would shake apart. As he watched Kiki leave, he started to gain some control on his musculature.

Jason walked back out of the mall. His Mom would be waiting for him by the Macy's entrance.

Jason perused the parking lot looking for his mother. He noticed an old gray Toyota swimming the parking lot. He flagged his Mom as she was about to drive past.

"Hi, honey!" His Mom was always so cheerful. "Did you have a good time?" Mom was oblivious about his little rendezvous.

"It was OK, I guess."

His Mom looked at him through the rearview mirror of the car. "Why are you smiling so much?"

A Writer's Recursion

The darkened room was aglow by the light emitting from the open laptop. The light was made more intense by the fact that what was displayed there was an empty word processing document with its completely white background. No text was evident on the screen. The cursor blinked on and off as the sole activity of the computer. It had been hours sitting idle. The light bathed the objects in the room, painting their shadows in a sharp relief against the living room wall.

He sat behind the laptop his head in his hands. He hadn't had an original thought in months. The deadline for his first draft had come and passed. His agent was getting very insistent that he produce something. Anything.

The writer rose from the desk and picked up his jacket from the chair by the hallway. Wrapping a thick woolen scarf around his neck, he ventured out of the apartment, down the stairs and into the street.

The street toughs and whores, who made up the bulk of the outdoors population this time of night, called to him as he headed down the thoroughfare to the corner diner. He cupped his hands to light a cigarette as he walked on. The warmth of the smoke heated his body in the cold night air. The blast of the nicotine in his blood gave him a surge of energy.

Dahlia was working tonight. He plopped down in a booth in her section. He had been working on her for weeks now, trying to get a date with her. No luck so far. He guessed she didn't have much use for broke writers. He would persist, however. Persistence was an asset to a writer. Persistence was a necessity, if he was being honest. He was.

Dahlia was his muse. She had inspired such of his works as, 'The Night Queen' and 'Bowling for Goodness Sake'. He placed his hands on the table of the booth and waited.

Dahlia was busy even at this time of night. She approached his table and hissed her usual greeting.

"What 'cha havin' honey?"

He knew the menu by heart. "Coffee. And a plate of eggs." He looked Dahlia in the eye. "And a slice of whatever it is you got goin' on …" He winked.

Dahlia sighed the sigh of a woman who had been harassed just one too many times. She noted the order on her order pad and turned to give it to the cook.

Waiting for the coffee and eggs, his thoughts went back to his days in school. How many times had he sat at the feet of his mentor, JE Moore, and talked about the process, about the work. Professor Moore had always insisted:

"Write what you know. Write about your life experience."

He would love to at this moment, he just didn't have the juice. Actually, he forgot to order juice. He waved Dahlia over. She brought him his cup of coffee.'

"Can I get an orange juice also, dear?"

"Sure, honey. Comin' right up." Dahlia ambled away. She did not look back. She did not look interested.

He ate his eggs and drank his juice. He lit a cigarette to enjoy with his coffee. This was one of the only places left in the city that looked the other way for smokers. He sat and cogitated his fate.

Maybe he should have been a lawyer like his Mom had suggested. Maybe he should have joined the Army like his Dad suggested. Maybe … His mind rambled with the lethargy of his body boosted by the kick start of the caffeine.

He paid his bill at the register and left a nice tip on the table. It was a nice tip for him. He really couldn't afford much. A short walk past the whores and toughs again placed him at his apartment door.

He closed the door to his apartment. There, on his desk, his laptop still shone bright. He pulled his desk chair back and sat. He would write what he knew. He would write from his life experience. Rolling to the desk and putting his fingers on the keyboard, he typed.

> ' The darkened room was aglow by the light emitting from the open laptop. The light was made more intense by the fact that what was displayed there

was an empty word processing document with its completely white background. No text was evident on the screen. The cursor blinked on and off as the sole activity of the computer. It had been hours sitting idle. The light bathed the objects in the room, painting their shadows in a sharp relief against the living room wall.

He sat behind the laptop his head in his hands. He hadn't had an original … '

Cultural Differences

The baggage claim at the airport was taking forever. Passengers from three flight were waiting by the carousel to retrieve their luggage. It had already been 30 minutes and still no activity on the moving belt, at all. People were sighing, loudly. Kids were growing impatient. Airport personnel hid as best they could. The mob was getting angry.

Charlie Mason folded his arms and resigned himself for a wait. It was his first time in Bucharest, and he resolved to go with the cultural flow. This was his vacation, after all, and he didn't want to spend it getting all uptight about every little thing. His patience would be rewarded. The conveyor belt started moving.

Charlie had graduated in the top of his class at Purdue in Mechanical Engineering. He made his living designing various parts for microwave ovens and other such small appliances, but what was his passion, nay his joy, was repairing old antique clocks. He had come to Bucharest to try and fix a clock tower in a small town in the north, Alba Mare, near the Ukrainian border.

Charlie grabbed his bag of tools and his backpack of clothing and headed for the rental counter. Surprisingly, they had his car waiting, and so he headed north to Alba Mare. The road was long and winding, but Charlie had not a care. The scenery was spectacular. He drove past high mountain lakes with rustic wooden barns dotting the hillsides. He beheld vast chasms between the mountains as he crested the ridges. He arrived at his destination tired from the driving, but in some ways refreshed.

The town square was deserted. In fact, the entire town seemed shut in for the night. Doors were locked. Windows shuttered. Not a sound could be heard, or a light seen. Alba Mare seemed for all intents deserted.

The cobblestone paving of the town square did nothing to diminish the feeling of history and tradition that oozed from the surrounding buildings. The town looked very much like a time capsule, not having changed much in hundreds of years. The buildings of the town square were constructed in what Charlie assumed was a timber frame structure. The facades of the edifices were done in lye-based cement for waterproofing. The town hall was the masterpiece of the town's architecture, ostensibly housing the town's government and, of note to Charlie, the town's clock tower.

Charlie took a moment to admire the clock in the town hall tower. From the design of the wrought iron he estimated 1600's. Maybe earlier. The face of the giant clock was done in exquisite stained glass. The multi-coloring of the glass gave the entire clock a regal countenance. Charlie knew why they wanted it refurbished. This unique time piece had no equal.

The Inn opposite the clock tower, the Corbentz, was to be his home while he was there. He lifted his bags from the trunk of the rental and approached the front door. He knocked. Nothing. He knocked again.

In time, a small crack appeared in the door. On the other side could be seen an older man with white hair. He whispered through the opening.

"Da?"

"I'm Charles Mason. I have a reservation?"

The old man closed the door. The turning of a great lock could be heard and then the door opened, allowing entry.

"Please, fast." The old man rushed Charlie into the hotel lobby. Once safely inside, the old man slammed the front door and relocked the mechanism.

Charlie was confused by the old guy's manner. He seemed afraid, but of what? He was a relatively harmless clock mechanic. There need be no worries. Oh well, Charlie chalked it up to another quirky Romanian cultural norm that Americans found hard to understand.

The old hotel keeper showed Charlie his room. It faced the town square and had an excellent view of the clock. Charlie tried to open the shutters of the window but found them firmly locked. The innkeeper placed a ceramic mug of actually quite refreshing ale on the nightstand.

"I fix in morning." The hotel manager nodded his head at the locked shutters and left.

The morning dawned and the noise in the town square woke Charlie from a dead sleep. The jetlag had not been kind. The villagers were assembling their market stalls on the cobblestones and purveying their goods for sale. The window in his room had become unshuttered and so Charlie could see the object of his restoration project. He decided to start right away.

Down in the lobby of the inn, an old lady who was the innkeepers wife, bent over from years of hard labor, was busy setting a table for breakfast. She motioned for Charlie to come eat. Charlie, not wanting to offend in any way, took a seat and beheld what was to be his meal.

The plate in front of him had been filled with bread and a cheese that he could smell before he could see it. Charlie diplomatically moved the cheese out of the way with his knife. A large cup of coffee accompanied the feast, which Charlie was much appreciative. Charlie ate his breakfast in silence.

Grabbing his bag of tools, it was only a short walk from the inn to the town hall. The great oaken door of the hall had been thrown wide, allowing access to the offices inside. Charlie tried to make sense of the signs on the walls, but not knowing the language, he became somewhat confused. A young lady approached.

"Pot sa tea jut?"

Charlie looked at her, helpless. "I'm afraid I don't speak your language."

"No problem. How I can help you?" The woman broke into English.

"I'm supposed to see your mayor this morning."

"Of course. Right this way please."

The young woman led him to a large office at the back of the building. She bade him sit in a chair in the outer office while she talked to the lady behind the desk. The lady picked up her telephone and, in time, a large man with even larger girth appeared.

"Mr. Mason, I presume?"

"Yes. Charlie, please."

"Charlie, then. Please, come right in." The mayor escorted Charlie into his offices.

The mayor's office was canvassed in wood paneling with abundant wood carvings. Over the paneling, great tapestries graced the walls, picturing all kinds of battles and hunting scenes. Charlie took a moment to consider the textile artwork.

"Exquisite." Charlie whispered the word.

"They depict some of the great moments in our history." The mayor beamed with pride at his collection.

"They are impressive indeed." Charlie inspected one of the tapestries closely. It pictured a man running from some kind of beast. The beast displayed razor sharp canine teeth. The man that was hunted was bleeding from his neck. Charlie thought the scene curious, but not to raise any uncomfortable questions, left the artwork uncommented upon.

The mayor began a mayoral dissertation about the history and tradition of their town. The town had been established in the 1400's and had survived eighteen wars. Charlie marveled at how long the mayor could speak. It seemed that he would never finish.

Finally, the mayor asked. "Shall we see the reason for your visit?"

"Yes, please." Charlie tried not to show his pleasure at the change of topic. It wasn't that Charlie was uninterested in the town's history, he was just eager to get started on the clock.

The spiral stairway outside the mayor's offices led upward to the clock tower itself. Charlie followed, his bag of tools in hand. Up three flights they went. Through a dusty wooden door, they entered the clock room. Charlie lay his bag down and looked. He rubbed a tear from his eye as he beheld the ancient structure. This was Charlie's finest hour in the clock world. This would be his greatest challenge.

Charlie went to work. He waved the mayor goodbye and spread his tools on the wooden floor of the clock room. The massive clockworks filled most of the room with small gangways providing access to all of its parts. Right away Charlie could see there were gears missing.

He pulled on the chains of the great weights that were provided to give the clock its power. The chains held tight. One thing he wouldn't need to fix, he thought.

There was a curious lever at the front of the mechanism. Charlie peered long and hard at the lever, not initially knowing what it might do. He studied the actuator with feverish intent when he jumped to his feet and exclaimed, "Aha!" Charlie pulled the lever and the great clockworks started moving. Charlie jumped to the platform below to watch, through a small pane of glass that had been strategically inserted in the stained-glass clock face. The hands of the clock on the outside were moving.

"Voila!" Charlie had solved the puzzle. The lever was a reset for the clock. The hands stood bolt upright at either noon or midnight depending on your reference.

He pulled his calipers out and started measuring all the gears. He needed very accurate numbers for these. The gear ratios determined the speed of the movement, which translated eventually to the movement of the minute and hour hands outside. The more accurate he could be at this stage would mean the more accurate a clock he could produce. And make no mistake about it, Charlie meant to produce one heck of an accurate clock.

It was about sunset when Charlie folded up all of the sketches and calculations he'd made for the clock. He needed to get to the car mechanic that the mayor had recommended to get some gears made. He also needed some gear shafts formed as some of the old wooden ones had splintered and cracked with age. He bundled up his tools and headed downward.

Charlie was met at the foot of the stairs by the innkeeper. The man was in an alarm.

"You come quick. We make dinner."

Charlie had a stop to make first. "I have to see the mechanic."

"He gone home. Everybody gone home."

Charlie looked around. All the buildings were closed and shuttered. It was a perplexing custom. He would have to see the mechanic tomorrow. "Ok."

Charlie ate his dinner at the inn. The old lady had prepared a roast of something with horns. And potatoes. It was surprisingly quite good, him not knowing exactly what he was eating. The entire repast was washed down with more of the quite refreshing ale.

Something was bothering him about the clock. He knew he had a good understanding of the workings that made the hands of the clock move to accurately measure time, but there were other workings. There were a set of gears that were intended to clang the big bell at the top of the clock tower at set times, twice a day. What was a mystery though, was the fact that the time of day changed every day. It was a poser for sure.

Charlie needed more ale if he was to solve this puzzle. The innkeeper and his wife had gone to bed, it was another of the delightful idiosyncrasies he had encountered on his trip. They truly loved their sleep. He being alone, he ventured into he kitchen for a refill of his mug. He would need a couple of more such trips before his bedtime.

After a week of fretting and tinkering, Charlie awoke to his last day fixing the clock. He needed to catch his flight the next day for home. After his breakfast of bread and a fried egg (he had asked for no cheese), he visited the mechanic to pick up his needed gears and such before heading to the town hall tower.

Charlie worked all day without stopping for anything. He needed to finish. He had to report back to work on Monday. The gears the mechanic had produced were of fine quality and slipped into their places quite readily. It wasn't long before Charlie was confident that he could restart the clock. Noon time came and Charlie pulled the stick he had used to halt the clock gears from moving and to his not so great surprise, the clock began tick, tick, ticking its way to 12:01.

Charlie clapped his hands in appreciation of the clock cooperating with his plans. He smiled wide. He beheld the handiwork of some long dead engineer that had been brought back to useful life. It did not get better than this for Charlie.

The only thing left for the Purdue engineer to tackle was the mechanism that rang the clock bell. He had thought about it often and deeply. He decided to do some experimentation on the mechanism.

Charlie took out his pad of paper yet again and began to take measurements at given intervals of the mechanism. He took data for hours. He knew the more data he had, the better he could discern its enigmatic pattern.

His cogitations were interrupted by the innkeeper. "Time to go. Dinner."

Charlie had not time to waste on things like eating. "I've still got work to do. I'll come soon." It was the best he could offer.

The innkeeper was insistent. "Please now. Dinner get cold."

"Soon. Soon." Charlie was already back lost in his bell ringing problem.

The innkeeper ran back to the inn.

The sun set and Charlie had an epiphany. The bell machine was using the position of the sun as its benchmark. Even more miraculous, it allowed for the movement of the earth around the sun. The bell would be rung one-half hour after sunrise and one-half hour before sunset every day. It would be rung early in the morning in summer and later in the morning in winter. It was a feat of mathematics, astronomy and engineering that Charlie had thought a man in the 1500's incapable. He regarded the accomplishment as quite ingenious.

Charlie quickly calculated the necessary setting for the mechanism to account for the current position of the Earth to the Sun. Satisfied with his math, he turned the gears to what he considered the correct positions and started the machine on its way. Charlie's time in Alba Mare was finished.

Charlie picked up his tools and was about to head for the stairs downward and to his dinner when he spotted a dark silhouette in the gangway just in front of him. He thought it might be the innkeeper. "Just finished. I'm coming now."

The dark silhouette walked into the moonlight shining through the stained-glass face of the clock. It was a man no doubt, and an old one. The man had long white hair that was thinning at the top. He lifted his hands to reveal long claw-like fingernails. His eyes were completely dilated showing only black emptiness where the iris should have been.

The old man hissed. In his hissing, he pulled back his lips to show a mouth full of razor-sharp canine teeth. Charlie thought back to the tapestry on the mayor's office. This must have been the beast depicted there. Charlie froze in fear. The fiend hissing at him showed no signs of anything other than pure hatred and lust.

The demon pounced on Charlie, snapping his teeth at Charlie's neck. Charlie responded reflexively, putting his left forearm in the way of the menacing teeth. The incubus bit down on Charlie's arm, hard. The pain of the bite filled Charlie's vision with the white noise of agony. Charlie thrust his attacker from his body with both arms.

The devil hissed his displeasure. He hissed it loudly. The fiend let out a high-pitched scream of vexation. The demon lunged a second time. Charlie's left forearm took yet another bite.

Charlie had had enough. Cultural norms be damned. This was unacceptable behavior in any society. The beast had gone way beyond the pale. Charlie balled his right hand into a fist and dealt the hissing wretch a blow to his nose.

The blow started a flow of black blood from the old man's nose. The angel of hell let out another scream, this time one of pain and suffering. The blow tottered the beast causing it to fall onto the platform below, where the rods that powered the hands of the clock pierced the face to move the minute and hour hands on the outside. The black bloodied interloper of the clock tower hit the stained-glass face of the clock and broke through. His head and shoulders faced the world outside.

What the demon had done unwittingly, however, in his attempt to steady his teetering body after Charlie's fist left him unstable, was to pull the reset lever of the clock. The actuator thrown, the hour hand moved in a clockwise direction, while the minute hand moved in counterclockwise to meet at midnight or noon, whatever your reference might be. When the clock hands met, they met the neck of the beast, severing his head from his body.

Charlie shook his head as he wrapped his jacket around his bleeding arm. He wasn't so much worried about his injury; he was hoping the decapitation hadn't hurt the clock. He unwrapped his tools and set about resetting the correct time for the clock.

The clock tower's ringing bell woke Charlie the next morning. He would need an early start if he was to make his flight. He washed and packed quickly and headed to the lobby. The old lady was laying out his breakfast.

"Just coffee this morning." Charlie was in a hurry.

Charlie said his goodbyes to the innkeeper and his wife. He picked up his bags and made for his rental car. To his surprise, the entire town was waiting by his car. They started to applaud him as he drew closer. Two of the men helped him put his bags in the trunk of the car.

Charlie looked up one last time at the clock tower. He checked the time with his watch. Perfection, 9:17 AM. It was then he noticed the head of the fiend he had encountered the night before stuck prominently on top of the pole that flew the town's flag. The devil still countenanced a vicious grin, his teeth bared in defiance even now.

Charlie smiled at the head on the pike. 'Another quirky Romanian custom.' Charlie shook his head at the comical amusement of it.

The townspeople cheered as Charlie drove away.

"What friendly folks!" Charlie waved to them.

Charlie vowed to return one day. He'd bring his own cheese, though.

Technological Barriers

You saw it everywhere. He saw it but he never realized what it was until he saw it in his wife. Now make no mistake, it affected him too, but to see it in his loved one made him pause. The thing was getting in the way. It was changing their lives. It had to be gotten rid of, or if not that, controlled. And, oh yes, he would control it. He would have it. He would see it die or he himself.

Gibson Carlyle sat at a candlelit table across from his wife, Madison, who was giggling at what she saw on her phone. Gibson took a fork and stabbed at the steak he had ordered. He might have stabbed a little too hard. His wife hadn't yet touched her Shrimp Diavolo. She would in time get to it, but now the phone was more important. Actually, the shrimp might have been more important than he himself at the time. Gibson called the waiter over and ordered another cocktail.

How many times had he wanted to grab the phone and throw it in the river? Or the lake. Or the trash. How many fantasies had he imagined of stomping the life out of the miniature computer and watching as the screen went black, ala the eyes of the Terminator? To say he loathed the machine was to underestimate the depth of his hatred and bile toward it.

The phone was his competition for his wife's affections, that was clear. He resolved to win her back.

The drive home was no different from dinner: he driving, and she glued to her phone. She would only pause to look his way and remark.

"Donna's daughter is pregnant!" She would beam with the news.

Or,

"Did you hear Harvey and Brianna are splitting up!?" Such juicy gossip needed to be shared to enhance the enjoyment.

Gibson would nod his head in acknowledgement, but he had learned long ago that a response was not necessary. She would be onto the next subject quickly and not able to process his comments let alone engage in meaningful conversation.

He clicked the garage door opener and guided the car into the garage. He pulled next to her car, the one with the dents in the bumpers and door from the various barricades and cars she had nudged and hit while peering into the vast wasteland of her phone. Yes, it was indeed time for an intervention. Gibson would see to it.

Madison was busy brushing her hair with one hand while reading her phone with the other. Gibson decided he had ample opportunity to surf the web to find a place for his phone offensive. He pulled up the coverage map of their provider and looked for places without coverage. There in glorious tan coloring was Montana. Up in the mountains. If only he could find a cabin or such to rent, his plan would have form. In minutes he had the email address of a landlord that offered such out of the way accommodations. What luck! Gibson booked a week in September. He texted his wife the details. It was the only way it would register with her.

September came and Gibson packed the car for the road trip. He called his wife to the car, and she followed her phone in hand. She took the passenger seat and reflexively, without much conscious thought, plugged her phone into the car's charger. Battery life was a big problem for her. The phone needed constant re-energization.

The drive would take most of the day. Gibson drove, lost in thought as he beheld the gorgeous scenery passing by the car. Desert turned to grassland which turned to mountains. His wife put her nose deeper and deeper into the handheld device. The stop for lunch progressed much as dinner had when he booked the trip. Gibson would be patient. He didn't want to spook her and tip his hand. No, this would just be a normal outing. A vacation of sorts. No need to feel anything out of the usual.

When they had reached the mountains, Madison noticed a marked dropping of the speed at which things would load. Before long the phone froze in certain apps.

"Hey! What gives!?" She looked at Gibson. "I've got no signal!"

"Probably just a temporary outage?" Gibson lied. He knew why her phone wasn't getting data.

They arrived at the cabin just as the sun was setting. The cabin was in actuality just a stick frame building covered in a plywood veneer that mimicked the look of a hardwood cabin. The inside was appointed with various pieces of used furniture and linens that gave the place a homey look. There was a single set of stairs, that were really more like a ladder, that led to the upstairs bedroom. The bedroom consisted of a bed and an end table, nothing more.

Madison had given up on getting any internet connection and instead had reverted to her go to game, 'Candy Crunch'. She played with a fever. Gibson drug the luggage inside the cabin to begin their woods retreat. Madison followed behind.

"I'm still not getting any signal…" She remarked to Gibson, like he was supposed to go get some signal or something.

Gibson had ripped the charger cord from the car and now cut the cable and threw it in the trash. He wanted nothing to lengthen his wife's withdrawal. She would need to go cold turkey if he was to have any success. The couple spent the rest of the night unpacking (her with one hand) and getting the cabin configured for their stay.

Climbing the stairs and jumping into the one bed the cabin offered, Gibson reached for the lamp on the side table. "Good night." He offered the sentiment he had so often offered at home. "Love you."

"Um hmm …" Madison offered her usual response.

It wouldn't be long, Gibson kept telling himself. The battery wouldn't last forever.

÷

The morning dawned with Gibson looking at a wife that seemed perturbed about something.

"It's dead."

Gibson had anticipated this. "What's dead?"

He knew, oh he knew. "My PHONE!" Madison was screaming. "My phone is dead, and I can't find the charger!"

Now Gibson had already destroyed the charger from the car, but what his wife didn't know was that he had taken her wall charger out of her luggage before they left. Her phone was dead, and it was going to stay that way for the foreseeable future.

"I'm sorry, honey." He wasn't.

Madison resumed her drug seeking behavior. She turned the entire contents of the luggage, what was left in there anyway, out onto the bed. Nothing. She ran down the stairs and visited the bathroom yet again. Nothing. She turned the kitchen upside down. She pulled the cushions out of the sofa and chairs. There was simply no way to charge her phone.

Madison screamed the anguished scream of the hopeless. Would she really have to endure the entire week up here without connection to her phone? The utter lack of stimulation! She would be bored. Probably for the first time in years. She needed her phone. Nay, she required it.

"What the heck am I supposed to do up here!?" She wailed at Gibson who had dressed and descended the stairs for breakfast.

"We could go for a hike?" Gibson was looking forward to that.

"Ugh!" Madison was not impressed. "Out there with the bugs!?" Madison found the nearest chair and slumped into it; the dead phone still firmly gripped in her left hand.

Gibson was starting to worry. He hadn't seen this side of his wife. She looked desperate and empty. Her eyes glazed over with a facial expression of woe and agony.

Later in the day, with dinner time ticking in his stomach and Gibson returning from his hike, he found Madison still slumped in the same chair. She hadn't showered or dressed. A slime of drool oozed from her mouth and down her neck. This was getting serious. Gibson decided a healthy dinner might brighten her mood. He pulled two frozen hamburgers from the cooler they had brought with them and took them outside to grill.

The landlord of the cabin had placed a metal grill in front of the cabin for just such feasts. Gibson collected some dead tree limbs from around the area and set them to blaze using a piece of newspaper as accelerant. In time he had a nice bed of red and white coals that would provide the searing the hamburgers required. He stepped away from the grill to retrieve a plate from the kitchen to transport his mahogany colored cow meat to the kitchen.

When Gibson returned to the grill, he was met by a visitor. The guest at the supper was a 1500-pound brown bear. The hungry Ursus Arctos had tipped over the grill and was busy gulping the hot seared hamburger down his gullet.

Gibson froze. Slowly, he backed away from the bear back into the cabin. Gibson reached for the door to close it to prevent entry by the huge bear, but the bear had another idea. The bear reared up on his hindquarters and pushed the door with all his weight. That weight was too much for Gibson and he fell over from the force of it.

The bear itself fell onto Gibson. Gibson tried to cry out, but the weight of the bear had emptied his lungs of air. He tried to get Madison's attention, but she just sat there, unmoving.

The bear now squarely inside the cabin, it began its perusal of the contents searching for anything remotely edible. The bear headed for the kitchen first. There were some nice smells coming that way.

Gibson picked himself off the floor and crawled to where his wife was still sitting. The incident of the bear rampaging through the cabin was having no effect on her. Gibson threw his wife over his back and slowly shuffled outside the cabin.

The sounds of glass breaking and pots and pans cascading to the floor echoed in Gibson's ears as he carried his wife down the mountain. He had to stop eventually; the weight of two people was too much for him to carry so fast for so long. He tried to wake his wife from her stupor.

"We've got to run. There's a bear."

Madison looked at him. "Huh?"

"There's a bear in the cabin!" Gibson's eyes were wide with fear.

"A bear." Madison scrunched her eyebrows to form a quizzical countenance.

"Yes! We have to go!" Gibson started pulling his wife along by the arm.

"There's a bear?" Madison was trying to get a grip on reality. "There is a bear." She got it. "We have to run!" Madison started pulling Gibson by the arm.

The couple ran down and down the side of the mountain. They had long since forsaken any kind of road or trail and soon found themselves lost.

Gibson turned to Madison. "We're lost."

"You think!?" Madison sighed. "Why are we even here in the first place?" She swatted a fly that was trying to have her skin for dinner.

"I thought we needed it." Gibson was through apologizing.

"Why in the world would we need this!"

It was a valid point. Being lost in the wilderness didn't seem so intelligent at the moment. "Whatever. Go back to your precious phone."

"I would IF I HAD A BATTERY AND ANY KIND OF SIGNAL!" Madison seethed.

Gibson decided to deescalate the argument. They needed to work together now. "Let's try and find the road. It's gotta be below us down there." Gibson pointed to the valley below.

The pair of bug bitten tourists gingerly felt their way down the mountain one foot at a time. The moonlight was little help illuminating the path, as the trees filtered most of it out. All at once, Madison stopped. She put her index finger to her lips.

She whispered, "You hear that?"

"Hear what?"

The couple stood still for a time until the sound presented itself again.

"Oooooooo …."

"Crap!" Gibson knew that sound. "Wolf! And close!"

The duo quickened their pace as the sounds of the wolves grew louder and louder. Madison imagined their hot breath on the back of her neck which gave her the motivation to get it going. Gibson needed no such imagery, he wanted off the mountain, now. Wolves had no mercy. Wolves would not be reasonable. Wolves take what they want.

They ran and stumbled and got poked by branches and a lot of skin came off in rubs and scrapes. They battled through underbrush and slipped on wet leaves and tumbled. In time, they came to a clearing of sorts. Gibson walked to the edge of the clearing and looked over the edge of a high cliff, standing over a river below.

"We're toast." He looked at Madison as if for the last time.

"That's it?" Madison didn't want to give up just yet.

Gibson knelt on one knee. He did so as much to increase his ability to think as his ability to replenish his body with the oxygen it had burned at so rapid a rate. He bowed his head. The wolves could be heard breaking through brush behind them.

"We'll have to jump."

"We'll have to what!" Madison wasn't convinced. She walked to the edge and saw the drop beyond. "Are you crazy!?"

"I'd rather have a broken leg than be eaten by wolves." Gibson had defined the dilemma.

The rustle in the bushes lining the clearing gave the alarm that the wolves had arrived. The sounds of low toned growling could be heard. If that hadn't been enough of a clue, the six pairs of yellow eyes staring out of the darkness should have alerted them. Gibson didn't hesitate, he grabbed Madison's arm and together they jumped off the cliff into the cold water below.

Gibson didn't know at first if he had been injured by the fall. The cold of the water felt like little needles of ice being driven into his skin. He swam for the surface of the water and gulped two lungs full of air. He looked for Madison, but she was not there.

"Maddie!" He tread the water even as it was hurling him downstream and over rocks and swirls. "Maddie!"

Madison, meanwhile, was fighting a battle of her own. She had survived the jump, but her ankle had become wedged in a tree limb. She fought for literally her life as she pushed hard on the limb with her free foot to try and lever the other out. It worked. She swam to the surface to find air and her husband.

The couple met midstream and grabbed hands. They let the current take them down and down. In time the current slowed to almost mothing as the river hit a level patch of terrain. Something on the upcoming bank caught Gibson's eye.

"Cabin!"

Husband and wife swam for the shore and pulled themselves up the bank. It was indeed a cabin and most welcome. They knocked at the door. Getting no answer, Gibson tried the knob. The door was unlocked. They entered and searched for the light switch. To their great delight, the lights worked.

Madison busied herself with the drying of their clothes over the wood burning stove they had lit, while Gibson rustled up some green beans and Spam he found in the cupboard. They sat by the stove and ate their meal.

Gibson was the first to speak. "You see that over there?"

"Um what's that?"

"I think it's a phone charger. You still got you phone?"

Madison hadn't thought about phones or anything else other than not being eaten in quite a while. She checked her shirt pocket then her pants pockets. There, in her back pants pocket, she found her phone. It was dripping wet.

"Let's try and dry it by the fire." Gibson pulled a chair close to the red-hot metal casing.

They sat in silence watching the fire burn and checking the phone from time to time turning it to dry all sides. Finally, when they thought it might be dry enough, they plugged it into the wall charger.

They watched for signs of smoke or electrical shorting. None were forthcoming. The phone just sat there; its screen painted that depressing black.

"C'mon baby, momma needs some help!" Madison tried to coax the inanimate piece of metal and plastics to life.

"C'mon, poppa needs a new pair of shoes!" Gibson wanted in on the action but could only paraphrase a popular witticism at the moment.

The phone was nonreactive. It lay dead as Marley's ghost. Until it didn't. The screen burst to light with a display of a red battery with blackness filling the inside.

"Haha!"

"Duuude!"

There were high fives and a little dancing at that development. In time, the OS booted, and the phone displayed the now most welcome information. It was those three little words Gibson had been waiting to hear. His dear wife spoke them.

"Emergency Use Only"

Madison was on it. She phoned 911.

÷

Having survived their ordeal in the wild, Gibson and Madison decided to dine out as a celebration. They picked their favorite restaurant and sat across from each other at their favorite table. The waiter brought some menus and lit the candles on the table.

"I'm feeling some wine tonight, you?" Gibson addressed his darling.

"I'm feeling two bottles!" Madison chimed in with her ideas.

The couple spent the evening eating and drinking and discussing the travails of their erstwhile vacation.

"You should have seen your eyes when the wolves howled!"

"You should have seen the bear when he about turned me into a carpet!"

They laughed.

On the way home Madison held Gibson's hand as he drove. As they turned onto the highway, Madison turned to her beloved as asked, "S'OK?"

Gibson kissed his wife's hand. "Sure."

Madison pulled her phone from its home in her purse and began to type full force with her two thumbs. She stopped mid message.

"Jamie Wilson broke her wrist bicycling!"

Gibson smiled. "Probably because of the little green men coming out of my ears."

"Um Hmm …"

He knew it wouldn't register.

The Vacation

The car was firmly packed full with luggage and children. A beautiful lady rode in the front passenger seat. The car sped down the highway. It was pointed beachward. The car would run all day and part of the night to get to the beach. It wasn't an option. To the beach they would go.

Dan Carter needed this vacation. The office had been a stress pit lately. He needed the quiet boredom of the beach with the constant droning of the pounding surf to calm his nerves. This vacation was to be a salve for his tired body. It was a therapy that no doctor had prescribed but with which no doctor would argue.

Dan Carter looked in the rear-view mirror. The next wave of fast-moving cars was approaching. He steeled himself for the frenzy that would follow their moving through his smaller, slower, automobile peloton on the road. The whoosh of each semi sent his little compact hatchback into a tailspin. The force of the wind generated by the mammoth eighteen wheelers was greater than the entire mass of his car, his family and his luggage. Gasoline included.

"I have to potty." Gerty was the first to draw bathroom-break blood. Gerty was his favorite daughter. His only daughter. She was so pure of heart and mind, unspoiled by a cruel and unforgiving world. At least, not yet. He slowed the car to find an exit.

Dan had anticipated the stop. Gerty had a bladder the size of a small undeveloped lima bean whose mother never loved it. As most eight-year-olds do. He had scheduled his own morning coffee to correspond with this first stop, so the break wasn't wasted. Dan pulled the car onto the exit ramp and prepared to slow and stop. There was a truck stop station at this exit. Dan drove there.

The kids piled out of the car looking for the giftshop. Dan's wife, Lori, grabbed Gerty's hand. "Let's find the bathroom."

Dan followed his son, Ryan, into the station. Ryan was his boy, his little man. Ryan too in many ways was still unspoiled by the worst of the world. He would have gladly given his life if it meant Ryan and Gerty would have a better life themselves. Dan never thought he could love anything that much, but he did.

Dan left his son browsing the biker paraphernalia to look for the coffee. When he rounded the donuts, he found the coffee array. The station boasted eight different kinds of coffee. Dan filled a cup with three of them. A little half and half later and Dan was at the cashier.

"Can I get one of these?" It was Ryan with two temporary tattoos in hand. One was a skull with the lettering 'Born to Ride' underneath. The other was a naked lady straddling a piston. Ostensibly, no other lettering or explanation was needed.

"We better go with the skull. Mom might have a problem with the pistons." Dan could be diplomatic when needed.

The Carter clan dove back into their little hatchback and started down the highway again. It wasn't long before Dan's concentration was broken again.

"Where are my sunglasses!?" It was Gerty again. "Mom, I lost my sunglasses."

"Did you look in your purse?" Mom was already unbuckling her seatbelt and folded over the seat into the back. Lori could find a wheat seed in a tornado, so Dan kept his eyes forward. Safety first.

"Here they are!" Lori pulled the glasses from under Gerty's teddy bear. Crisis averted.

Dan fought the fight with the traffic on the highway while his family snored inside the car. The coffee helped keep his eyes open and the car between the white lines. There were several more stops for potty, snacks, lunch, giftshops, gasoline and more coffee. In time the Carter family arrived at their hotel, the car full of gas station giftshop items and dreams of a relaxing vacation by the sea.

The next morning the family arose to a glorious sun filled day. Dan was the first to the beach, carrying a large cooler full of rehydration fluids. Lori and the kids followed, they had paused at the street between their hotel and the beach to let the cars pass. Dan put the cooler down and approached the young lady setting up umbrellas on the beach.

"So, you must be the lady that's renting beach umbrellas?" Dan shaded his eyes from the sun, still low in the sky.

"Yes, that's me!" The girl continued with her labors, the umbrellas were large and unwieldy.

"I'm interested in one umbrella and two lounge chairs for the week." Dan started to pull his wallet out of his swimming trunks.

"Sure. It's $200 for the week."

Now two hundred dollars was a significant portion of Dan's assumed budget for the vacation, but he longed for the relaxation the lounge chairs in the shade of an umbrella could give. He had brought a book with him to read between naps and he felt the price a good value for all that it provided. He handed the money to the young woman.

"Take that one over there." The woman pointed to a set of chairs under an umbrella already setup and ready to go.

Dan pulled the cooler with him to his home for the week. Oh, the book. Oh, the sound of the surf. Oh, the sea gulls, the smell of the saltwater. Why oh why had they ever left the beach!? Life was so easy here. So simple, so perfect.

Dan nestled into one of the chairs and grabbed his book from inside his beach towel.

The wife and kids arrived. Lori assumed her place in the other lounge chair and started applying sunscreen to herself and the kids. The kids looked at the ocean. The looked at each other. They looked at their Dad.

"What do we do now?"

Dan looked at his children. He was a bit perplexed. They were at the BEACH! What could they ever want more? "Go. Run. Play. Swim."

The kids ambled off toward the water. Dan opened his book and began to read. It was a murder mystery. Delicious!

After a while, Dan was interrupted by a pair of children plopping themselves down in front of his chair.

"We're bored."

Dan looked up from his book. He looked over to his wife who was smiling from ear to ear.

"You're bored?"

The kids nodded in assent.

Dan closed his book. It was time for some real Dad time. Dan would teach them in this moment. Boredom was impossible at the beach. "You guys ever body surfed?"

"What? No."

Dan led his kids to the sea. The winds were high and the surf as well. The waves were topping four feet. It was perfect for body surfing. Dan took his brood into the water.

"Now do what I do, OK?"

"OK."

"When a nice wave comes along you throw yourself into its flow, just in front of it. Like this."

Dan dove headfirst into the water, allowing the wave to keep his body moving all the way into shore. He stood up when his momentum stopped, but not before the water forced his bathing suit to his knees. Dan nervously grabbed his suit and pulled it back on. The kids giggled.

"There. You try it!"

The kids tried throwing themselves in front of their waves with little success. They hadn't yet gotten the rhythm right where the wave could propel them forward.

"Keep at it!" Dan went back to his lounge chair, confident that the kids would be caught up in the surfing fever he had caught so early on in his youth.

He had no sooner sat down on the chair, but he heard his daughter's voice. "Ryan almost drowned."

Dan looked over and there was his son coughing up sea water. He called the boy over and began to comfort him. "What happened?"

"The wave pulled me under."

The surf was awfully steep, Dan had to admit. These were little kids not a grown-up adult like he himself. Maybe he had misread their ability to handle such powerful water.

"Surf's too high. Maybe it will slow down and we can try again?"

Ryan didn't look like he wanted to try again. Gerty had taken to her mother and was laying on the chair beside her. Dan went back to his book, hoping that if he ignored the situation, it might go away. In time, he heard the chorus that he had heard a thousand times.

"We're bored."

"Find something to do!" Dan knew that there were times for tough love in life, and by gum now seemed like one of those times.

The kids stomped off to go sit by the shore. Dan went back to his book, but something wasn't right. He could feel a cold dark stare falling on his body. He looked up and sure enough, there it was. Lori was looking at him with a disappointed expression on her face.

"It's their vacation too, you know."

Now Dan was a dedicated family man. If his family wasn't happy, he wasn't happy. He called the kids over.

"OK, what do you guys want to do?"

"We want to go swimming at the hotel pool."

Here they had an entire ocean to swim in and explore and all they wanted to do was to swim at the postage stamp sized pool at the hotel. It boggled Dan's mind. But, if that's what they wanted, he would accede.

"OK, let's go."

The kids jumped for joy. Lori smiled, the said, "Take the cooler, they need to stay hydrated."

"What 'bout you?"

Lori pulled her thermos of water from behind her lounge chair and in a totally passive aggressive manner wiggled it from side to side as much to say, 'I've got it, idgit.'.

<÷>

The hotel pool was deserted. All right-thinking families were enjoying the day at the ocean's edge. Dan set down the cooler and pulled up one of the plastic lounge chairs provided for such activity. The plastic stuck to his flesh. It gave an unpleasant sensation, probably to disincentivize folks from tarrying too long at the pool. Too many people at the pool meant they had to maintain it more often.

Dan pulled his book out from his beach towel and resumed his mystery novel. The entire Thornton family was gathering at the old man's mansion on the slopes of the Outer Hebrides. The rain was coming down in sheets. Murder must be in the air. Dan's face sparkled with the intrigue.

"We want you to swim too!" Gerty was pulling his arm. She could be very persuasive normally, but her obvious insistence meant resistance to be futile. Dan pulled off his t-shirt and dove into the water.

The kids' favorite game in the pool had always been, 'Let's drown Dad'. Today would be no different. The two ganged up on Dan and soon had him at the bottom of the shallow end with both standing on him to complete the homicide.

Dan would go along with the ruse, playing dead, until he couldn't hold his breath any longer. Then there was a price to be paid for trying to drown old Dad. Dan raised like Godzilla from beneath the surface and would swim after the perpetrators of the heinous crime, his fingers coiled in claw-like fashion, should he be lucky enough to grab one of them.

The kids screamed their delight.

<÷>

When Lori arrived at the pool, Dan and the kids were lounging dead on the lounge chairs. Even the kids had exhausted, what seemed to her and her husband as an endless supply of energy. Lori plopped down on a chair next to Dan.

"You guys eaten anything today?"

Dan turned over to face his wife. He looked like a man defeated. He mumbled something but Lori couldn't quite make it out. Dan muttered again.

"Fooood."

The family washed and changed clothes and met at the car in the parking lot. Dan kicked the car to life, and they were off.

"Where are we going?" Gerty always wanted to know.

"A great big surprise!" Dan always liked to surprise his family.

The Carter's ended up at Captain Jack's Seafood restaurant and Laundromat. It had great Yelp reviews and the landlocked Carter's loved fresh seafood when they could get it. Dan sidled up to the hostess to see if they could get a table.

"Four for dinner."

The seventeen-year-old hostess looked through her appointment book. "Do you have a reservation?"

Dan was crestfallen. The lack of a reservation usually meant the waiting list.

"Umm no. We thought it being this early in the evening we might get lucky."

"Name?" The girl had heard it all before even at such a young age.

"Carter."

"It'll be about 15 minutes."

"Ugh."

Dan returned to his family. He hadn't been able to win a table for his brood. The hunting expedition had failed. They would have to sit and wait for the mercy of the seventeen-year-old. They found the corner of a bench already filled with other folks waiting.

"There's table right there!" Gerty stated the obvious.

"There's two more over there!" Ryan was hungry.

Not wanting to feel the wrath of the young girl at the hostess station, Dan cautioned his kids to keep their voices down. Riling the hostess could add minutes or even hours to their wait time.

"Those tables don't have a waiter yet." Dan made an excuse. He didn't know if it was actually true, but it sounded good. The result was two relatively quiet kids with empty stomachs and raging attitudes.

Fifteen minutes came and went. Dan was getting nervous. He had so far prevented the entire meltdown of the kids, but he knew like any pressure cooker when the lid came off all kinds of nastiness could ensue. He visited the Hostess.

"How are we doing?"

"Umm … let's see … what was your name again?"

"Carter."

"Yes, here you are. You're number ten in line. It won't be long."

Dan returned to the family.

Lori spoke first. "We should have brought our laundry!" She smiled.

Lori was always the optimist. Dan brought her back to Earth. "We're tenth in the queue."

Another fifteen minutes went by. Lori decided to check with the hostess this time. The answer – Tenth in line.

"Are you kidding me!?" Dan was about to lose it. "We were tenth fifteen minutes ago!"

Dan steeled himself for the confrontation he would now have to endure on his supposed relaxing vacation. He would have to be firm with a seventeen-year-old then argue with her twenty-two-year-old manager. He stiffened his collar and approached the hostess' station.

"You said it was going to be fifteen minutes a half hour ago."

The hostess looked at Dan. "What was your name again?"

"My name. As my name has always been. IS... CARTER." Dan stared her straight in the eye.

"Let's see. Oh, there you are. You're number ten. It won't be long."

"We've been ten for a half hour!!"

"Um hmm ..." The hostess was unimpressed. She had had to deal with tourists all her seventeen years and she really didn't give a toss.

"I want to talk to the manager." Dan hated to have to escalate the problem, but this wasn't working.

"Sure. One moment please."

The girl left Dan at the hostess station while she went into the kitchen. She returned after a cigarette's worth of time and immediately started looking at her book. She said nothing about the manager.

Dan looked at her with an evil intent. How his evening would go would not be determined by an adolescent. No, he would take the high road. If not for himself, for his family. It was quite possible that this little drama was playing out at all of the restaurants in town. No, he needed to be patient. He turned and walked away.

Fifteen minutes later, Dan heard those words he had longed to hear.

"Carter, party of four."

Dan ran to the hostess station.

The hostess looked past him for the Carter party.

"That's me… ?" Dan gave the girl a quizzical look. Did she really not know him, or was she playing some kind of passive aggressive game. He decided it might be the latter.

The hostess showed the Carter's to their table by the kitchen. Dan was going to complain, but experience told him that would only get them another waiting time in line. He decided to try and make the best of it. Dan was hungry and he worried the children might just pass out soon.

"What a great table! We're right by the kitchen. Our food will be extra hot when we get it!" He winked at the kids who by now had lost all sense of humor.

A waiter came to the table bearing four glasses of water and three menus. "I'm Tom. I'll be right back." The waiter was gone before they could even say a proper hello.

The menu featured all kinds of delicacies from the sea. There were deep fried mussels. Deep fried haddock. Deep fried shrimps. Yes, shrimps. Deep fried potatoes and even deep-fried dough (hush puppies). Dan's stomach turned. It didn't do well with deep fried food, period.

In time, the waiter decided to come back for their order. Lori ordered the shrimp salad. It was probably the healthiest item on the menu. The kids got Captain Jack's deck hand meal for 'all the little ones'. Dan opted for the fried haddock and coleslaw. He reasoned he could decrust the fish to make it less greasy. The waiter wrote in his book and left.

The Carter family slumped in their chairs. They had had a busy day and without the fuel that comes from food, their tired bodies refused to work properly. Dan tried to amuse them with his puppet show of knifey and forkey. His attempts at jocularity fell on deaf ears.

Dan rubbed his stomach, his GERD was acting up, he needed to eat something, anything to sop up the excess acid being produced.

Fifteen minutes later. Why did it always seem like it took fifteen minutes to do anything here? Anyway, fifteen minutes later the food arrived. The waiter apologized to Lori; they were out of shrimps. Yes, shrimps. So, they had substituted two large lobster tails in her salad. The kids had been upgraded from deck hand status to crewman which involved adding a third chicken finger and onion rings with their fries. The waiter plopped Dan's plate in front of him.

Now what had been described as delicious haddock crusted in a light breading looked suspiciously a lot like fish sticks. The onion rings that accompanied them were soaked in grease. Dan's stomach clenched at seeing the greasy food. It would not be pleasant should he consume it.

Dan tried scraping the breading from the fish. The bulk of the fish sticks were breading, however. He did manage to scrape one side and them with his fork pull the little actual fish that was there into a tiny lint ball to eat. It was better than nothing. Not much better, but better.

The onion rings could not be eaten at any cost. Dan cracked them open and pulled the little string of onion on the inside out and ate that. When he was finished, he had a plate of breading bits left. He was still hungry. It was then he saw the crackers the waiter had left in the middle of the table. Dan pounced before anyone else noticed and shoved the crackers into his mouth.

<÷>

The next morning, Lori threw a brochure in front of a still waking Dan and his coffee. It was an advert for the Seven Flags amusement park in the neighboring county.

"I thought we could take the kids there today. They would love it."

Now the amusement park was an expense that Dan had not counted on. Dan had planned on spending his vacation laying on the beach, reading and relaxing. He had already spent $200 to reserve his seat there. This was an unneeded expense.

"Umm, I thought we were going to go to the beach?"

"You don't really think they'll put up with that do you?"

Dan remembered the day before when they had been so bored and Ryan almost drowned. He remembered the words of his wife that, 'it was their vacation too'. Dan clothed himself for the amusement park.

Dan was nursing a stomachache accompanied by a headache. He reached inside his jacket pocket and produced a bottle of aspirin. He took two. Actually, three was better. The family arrived at the Seven Flags and immediately the kids started running for the rides.

Lori and Dan held back and let their offspring run wild a bit. They felt relatively safe inside the confines of the park, but they would keep a sharp eye out for any trouble. They found an empty bench and decided to sit and take in the sights and sounds of the park.

There were rumbles of roller coasters speeding down their tracks followed by the screams of their passengers. A man was operating a weight guessing booth. For one dollar he boasted he could guess your weight within five pounds. If you won, you'd get a stuffed animal made in China that he bought for thirty-nine cents.

There were the smells. Cotton candy was being spun. Pretzels being baked. The was a booth setup with a teenager stirring a deep vat of caramel popcorn. Dan decided on the popcorn. He returned to his bride, with a large bag.

"Have some?"

"Umm, yes please!" Lori picked two pieces from the top.

Dan was about to indulge when some familiar voices could be heard to his right.

"We want to go on the Dancing Demon!" It was the kids. The Dancing Demon was the largest coaster in the park.

"Well, what's stopping you?" Dan started to munch on his popcorn.

"We want you to go with us!"

Now Dan was still nursing his head and stomach aches. He didn't think a rollercoaster, let alone a Dancing Demon, was the thing right now.

"Take your Mom."

Lori turned to him and gave him one of her looks. It conveyed a message of 'you have got to have gone completely insane'.

"She's too scared." The kids knew their Mom. She would freak out on the escalator at the mall.

Lori spoke. "C'mon, I'll hold your popcorn for you."

Reluctantly, and he meant reluctantly, Dan grabbed his kids' hands and made for the waiting line for the Dancing Demon.

The sign at the beginning of the line to board the coaster said, 'Two hour wait from here.' Dan was glad when they passed that up. He would be less happy, however, when at the next turn the sign said, '90-minute wait'. He decided to power through, though. His kids were energized and anxious, anticipating the death defying stunts yet to come.

The ninety minutes passed quickly enough, and the trio were allowed entry onto the coaster. The seats were four across, so they happily sat down beside each other. There was a harness of sorts that they pulled over their heads and onto their chests. The head rests had these curiously padded sides. Dan wondered why they had padded sides. He had never seen that in a roller coaster before.

All strapped in, the coaster left the station. It slowly climbed a very high hill. Dan had seen this before; it was gathering potential energy for the trip through the rest of the structure. They crested the hill and started to fall.

Now what transpired after that was a blur to Dan. He would remember the twists and turns and how the g forces kept punching the sides of his head back and forth inside the headrest with the padding. 'Oh, that's why.' Dan had found the reason for the padding.

Gerty and Ryan were screaming with delight. They took every twist as a joy, every turn as an adventure. Dan was having a totally different experience. Dan was having a medical crisis of sorts. It wasn't his heart. It was his stomach.

The ride stopped and Dan immediately emptied his stomach contents on the platform beside the coaster. Gerty stepped over it but not before giving the requisite 'ewwww'. Ryan laughed.

Back at the bench with Lori, Dan gulped down three more aspirin. He knew he was overdosing, but his headache had gone from being bad to raging evil. The aspirin seemed to be helping a bit but he was thinking more aspirin might be in his future. Lori offered him his caramel popcorn. Dan turned sideways and dry heaved.

"Let's go again!" Ryan was pulling his Dad forward to the Dancing Demon.

"Yes, Daddy let's go again!" Gerty joined in.

Lori looked at her husband. He looked so bad, so sick, she felt sorry for him. But when she saw the look of resignation come over his face and him ambling slowly to the roller coaster line she had to laugh.

<÷>

One of the things that Dan's family before Lori had always loved was fishing. Dan was no exception. He wanted his kids to learn to love it too. That's why the next day he surprised them all by taking them to the pier to do some pier fishing.

Dan led his brood up to the fish house at the entrance to the pier and approached the teenager at the cash register. The youth was busy texting, so Dan had to wait for the conversation to end. It took a while.

"We want to fish."

The kid looked up from his phone. He pointed to the piece of paper nailed to the post by the register. It had all the prices listed.

Pier fishing license $15

Sardines $8

Live bait $14

Dan perused the list. They were going to need poles and tackle. "How much for the fishing poles and tackle?"

"$15 per pole."

"OK. We need 4 licenses, 4 poles, and two packages of sardines."

The kid sighed and begrudgingly toted up the order on the register. "$146"

Dan had gotten a total of $136. He brought it to the lad's attention. The kid went back through the paper tape that he had produced when the transaction was keyed in. He got to the line that listed the $10 new account fee.

"$10 new account." He showed Dan the entry.

Dan shelled out the money. It was a bit more than he had budgeted to spend. Heck he was already way over budget, what was a little more?

Dan and family took their spot along the railing way out toward the end of the pier. Dan wanted deeper waters. Bigger fish tended to swim deeper waters. He hooked up the poles and gave them to the kids.

"What do we do with these?" The kids were baffled.

"Take a frozen sardine out of the package and hook it on your hook. Look, like this." Dan baited the first line.

Ryan grabbed a slimy fish out of the package and tried to hook it. He ended up putting the sharp end of the hook in his finger. "Ouch!"

Lori jumped on the problem. She grabbed a tube of Neosporin out of her handbag and applied it liberally to Ryan's wound. "He's just a kid!" She leered at Dan. "We want the sardine on the line, not Ryan, right!?"

Dan stopped what he was doing and baited Ryan's line. He had already helped Gerty get her line in the water and was about to bait his lovely wife's hook when Gerty screamed, "It's pulling me in!"

Dan jumped for Gerty's pole before the fish drug her over the side and helped her reel it in. When they had it on the deck of the pier, they could see Gerty had caught a rather large clam. Dan took the clam off the line and threw it back in the water. He then recast Gerty's line.

Dan went back to help his wife, but she had already cast her line. It was Dan's turn to get in the water. Before he could get a sardine out of the bag, Ryan called out. "Fish on!' Ryan had heard that on TV.

Ryan had hooked a small remora. It was one of those alien looking fish with a sucker on top of their head that attach them to the underside of a shark. They then eat the stuff that falls out of the shark's mouth. The kids exclaimed their disgust at the ugliness of the fish. "Ewwww."

By the time Dan had unhooked the remora and sent it back to Davey's Locker, Lori had something. Gerty had pulled her line out of the water and her sardine was gone. Ryan wanted another sardine on his line to try and get another of those ugly remoras.

Dan worked with a frenzy to keep lines baited and fish unhooked and back in the ocean. It seemed every time he thought he might have some time to bait his own line, he had another emergency with someone else's line. This went on for hours until finally the sardine bait was gone, and the kids had lost interest in fishing, and truthfully so had Dan.

Dan gathered their gear to return it to the pier house.

<÷>

The next day dawned to a beach soaking in rain. Dan looked out from the hotel window to see the rain coming down. There would be no beach today. The kids were busy watching Square Bob with Spongey Pants on the TV. No beach today, but that still meant he could get to his book finally.

Dan rifled through his beach towel and belongings searching for the mystery novel. It just wasn't to be found. He thought back in his mind to the events of the last days. The last time he had seen the book was for sure at the pool. Maybe the book had been given to the hotel's lost and found. He beelined for the lobby.

The teenager at the front desk greeted Dan as he approached. "Good morning!"

Dan answered the cheerful lad. "Yes. Except for the rain." Dan scowled. "Do you have a lost and found?"

The boy reached under the desk and produced a cardboard box full of items. There were sunglasses, swimming trunks, sunscreen and various beach toys. "You lookin' for something in particular?"

"I lost my book. 'Prognosis Murder'"

"Let's see..." The hotel host dug deep into the box. "Aha! Here it is." He showed the book to Dan.

Dan perused the cover of the book. It displayed a hunky guy with his shirt torn apart, revealing a washboard stomach. There was a woman at his feet desperate to pull him close to her. The title, 'Hot Summer', left Dan less than enthusiastic about reading it.

"Nope. Not it."

Dan returned to the room downhearted. The Square Bob Spongey Pants marathon was in full swing on the TV. Lori had pulled out a magazine from her luggage and was reading it on the bed. Dan went back to the window. Maybe the rain would stop, and he could go back to his comfy lounge chair on the beach. It was then the Square Bob was interrupted by an Emergency Broadcast Message.

"Hurricane warning for Hopson Beach and Newport Royal. Residents are advised to evacuate immediately. High winds and rising surf will cause serious threat to life and property."

"What do they mean hurricane?" Ryan asked his Dad.

"It's going to get really windy and wet." Dan knew the dangers of a hurricane. His parents had waited one out when he was young, and it had destroyed most of their house. It was not fun at all.

"Let's pack. We gotta go."

The Carter's packed with alacrity and were soon ensconced in the car and headed out of town, back home. They had no sooner turned the corner from the hotel when they met a traffic jam. It seemed that everyone was leaving the beach at the same time.

Little by little, inch by inch, they made their way out of town. The rain began to start falling more horizontally than vertically as the winds picked up strength. The little hatchback buckled with each gust. Dan kept his eye on the road ahead. Even at such low speeds, he was having trouble keeping the car straight.

In time, the Carter's made the highway and began the long journey home. It would be well past midnight before they opened their front door and fell into their abode. Dan carried the kids to their bedrooms.

"They look so angelic when they sleep." Lori hugged her husband as he turned off the lights in Gerty's room.

Dan hugged his wife back. They walked to their room, each trying to hold the other upright, they were dead tired.

"Sorry it wasn't what you wanted for a vacation, honey." Lori kissed her man as she turned to go to sleep.

Dan thought back to the swimming in the pool, the roller coaster and the fishing. He had spent time with his kids and wife. Not much could beat that.

"Probably the best vacation of my life." Dan rolled over and in seconds was fast asleep.

The Gargoyle

The bell on the front door of the shop clinked. A customer entered. It had been awhile since anyone had ventured into his little store. Probably some octogenarian looking for a bit of nostalgia. People these days were only interested in the new and the now. His old dusty antiques were anathema to an internet generation. New, or newly refurbished were the order of the day.

The lady customer was dressed in a thick overcoat with a silk scarf as adornment. She smelled of rich perfume. Not anything off the shelf, something exotic. She clopped forward to his desk in the back where he spent most of his days. The sound of her high heels beat a rhythmic staccato on his wooden floors. She carried with her a rather large bag that held something heavy. She labored as she lifted the bag onto his desk.

Without a word, she opened her bag and produced the object of her visit. She unwrapped the stone artifact that was hidden by a cloth to reveal a rather grotesque figure. The piece was carved marble. He picked up the item in his hands and began to roll it around to apprise its value. He knew she wanted to sell it. That was mostly the reason for his visitors these days.

"Do you know what you have here?" He always wanted to start his negotiations getting them to reveal something he could use to barter.

"Gargoyle. Seventh century."

He rolled the stone demon around some more. She probably was right. The aging on the marble looked right. There were no markings of modern tools. "Probably Turkey. Or father east." He gauged the origin of the piece from his knowledge of Asian art.

"You know your stuff. It was my father's." She finished taking off her leather gloves. "I'm looking to sell it."

Now the money phase of their little tête-à-tête was to begin. He pretended to look closer at a mark on the gargoyle with a magnifying glass. "How much were you thinking?" It was always best to have them give the first number.

"One thousand." She looked resolute. "I'm taking a trip."

That sounded a little like an ultimatum to him. One thousand dollars for such an important and well-preserved specimen was a steal and he knew it. "Ok." He went to the back room and got the cash out of his safe.

He counted out ten one-hundred-dollar bills for the lady and she stacked them and folded them into her purse. She put her gloves back on and buttoned her coat tight against the cold outside. "Good luck."

She had said the words with a note of somber sorrow. It was more of a warning to his ears than a wish for good fortune. Whatever her problem, he knew he had made the buy of his year. He would profit greatly from the purchase. This was museum quality merchandise. He picked up the gargoyle and placed it in the glass case beside the desk where he kept his most valuable pieces. He took a moment to look at the beastly countenance that had been carved on the face of the devil. Whoever made this artifact wanted to instill fear in the beholder. His work was still inspiring that fear to this day, he mused.

He sat at his desk regarding the stone demon. The gargoyle with its wide eyes, flared nostrils and bared teeth glared back at him. The beast had horns, much like a ram he thought. It boasted sharp pointy ears and two wings. The wings reminded him of a bat with the fleshy veiny skin between long slender bones.

The day lingered on with no further customers. The shop was struggling, no customers meant no income, meant eventual bankruptcy. He decided to close early. There had been a great buy that day. No need to push it. He locked the front door and made his way to the back room where his living quarters were.

He opened the case. He had to feel the thing again. If for nothing else, to make sure it was really real. He picked the heavy object up and rolled it over again and again, looking for flaws or defects. No, the ancient artifact was just what he had suspected. He was mystified by the gargoyle. The weight of history began to hold him in a devotion for the object. The marble carving was becoming something more than mere stone.

Just for fun, he loaded up a web site on his laptop, that he perused from time to time. It was an auction house that specialized in ancient antiquities. He searched and scrolled through dozens of pages. They had nothing even close to what he had sitting in his glass case. He would be a rich man indeed.

He fantasized about the windfall. He would sell the shop as well and retire to an island in the Mediterranean. He loved that part of the world. He didn't know if his gargoyle would bring enough money to fund that, but it was fun to dream a little. He turned off the lights and withdrew to his private rooms.

÷

When he opened the shop the next day he was met by his neighbor at the front door. The man was frantic. He waved for him to hurry in unlocking the door. There was important news to be shared. He unlocked the door.

"Did you hear?" The neighbor asked wide eyed.

"Hear what?"

"The murder!? They found a hooker in the alley between some dumpsters. She was gutted like a wild animal."

"Really? How gruesome."

The pair of shop owners walked to the end of the block where the police had set up their barriers. The street was blocked with several police cars, their lights flashing. He craned his neck to peer into the alley. The coroner was there bagging up the remains. His assistant was washing the area to alleviate a biohazard in the area.

It was cold. He pulled his cardigan close and tightened his tie. This would not be good for business. The coroner's assistant pushed the gurney with the bag of remains past them. He recognized the shoe they had placed on top of the bag. She had worked their street for quite a while.

Having had enough of the drama for today, he ventured back to his little shop. The bell on the front door would ring like it used to when he first opened the shop. It was mainly for folks wanting to use the bathroom, but it reminded him of better days.

He was about to close for the day when a last visitor graced his threshold. It was Anderson, from Anderson Antiques. The man was his competition in the area.

"Quite the excitement over here, eh?" Anderson had come to gloat.

"Yes. Very grizzly." He faced he man with dispassion on his face.

"Had much business from the increased traffic."

"Mostly just lookie lous and people needing to pee."

"Shame." Anderson started to peruse his inventory. "Say, this is a nice piece. Louis XV I believe?"

"Yes. I'll give you a good price on it." He winked at Anderson. The wink was one of challenge not humor.

"Umm… Let me think on it." Anderson left.

He went back to his desk. The gargoyle was sitting in its place in the glass case, but something was different. The door to the case was slightly ajar and there was something staining the piece. He opened the case door and fondled his prize. What was that brown substance on it?

Not to ruin the patina of the artifact, he took a damp linen rag and gingerly started to work on the stain. It came free from the marble readily. When he had completely cleaned the stone devil he stepped back at the sight of the linen. It looked like he had just cleaned a wound. Could the substance be blood? How did it get there?

He put the demon back in the case and closed the door again. He latched the latch. He had had enough excitement for one day, what with the murder and the bloody gargoyle. 'Could they be related?', he thought. He laughed. He was letting the little marble creature influence his thinking. He retired to his bed chamber.

÷

Day dawned again and he woke to open the store. The street was deserted as normal. He unlocked the front door and went back to his desk. He stared at the stack of bills in the box on his desk. If things didn't change and soon, he'd have to close the shop. He couldn't imagine what kind of change would even allow him to stay open. He poured a cup of coffee and checked the news the internet.

It seemed there had ben a second homicide in the city. The details appeared as gruesome as the first. This time it was an antiques dealer who had fallen prey to the killer. A man named Anderson. He bristled at that. He had just seen him the day before.

He was conflicted. The man Anderson had been a loathsome, aggressive, money grubbing pain in his back for years and so he would not mourn him leaving. On the other hand, the man had met a cruel fate. He read onward.

It seems the murderer had eviscerated Anderson as well. Just like the hooker. The police had named it a serial killing. They searched a single perpetrator for both crimes. It seemed that both victims had had their hearts removed. The organs could not be found at the scene.

Something rhymed about this second murder. He leaned back in his chair and looked at his gargoyle still sitting in the glass case. The case was ajar as before. He had latched the case the night before. He was certain about that. He had made a special effort to do it.

He opened the case and pulled the marble statuette out. There streaked all over the piece were the brown stains of before. He got his cloth from the bathroom and started to clean again. It was blood. There was no doubt about it.

His mind ran wild. How could it do it? Why did it do it? It was preposterous but there it was right in front of him. There was a stone devil that seemed to like bathing itself in blood. He couldn't get past those facts.

He formulated a plan. He would get a nanny cam and put it on his desk. He would videotape the comings and goings in the room to find out what exactly this demon from the underworld was doing at night. A visit to the electronics store later and he was setting the camera on the desk with full view of the glass case.

He fretted the entire day. What had he gotten himself into? It seemed impossible. He reassured himself that he was just imagining things and that the next day the nanny cam would verify that all his thoughts had just been paranoia.

÷

The next day he woke early. He was eager to view the nanny cam footage. He dressed quickly and combed his long hair. The nanny cam was still in its place on the desk. The gargoyle was covered in blood as before. He powered up his laptop to view the video of last night.

The video started off rather boring. Nothing happened. The camera faithfully recorded a marble statuette sitting in a glass case. He decided to fast forward. Maybe he could still catch what had happened even at the more rapid rate. He watched on.

The recording ticked off the hours, one by one. No movement. Then, about three AM according to the log, something happened. Slowly a man started to enter the frame. The man looked familiar to him. He had blood all over his hands and he carried something in his right hand. He opened the bottom drawer of the desk and plopped the item there.

The man had a moustache and long brown hair. It was a moustache that he had combed many, many times. He would recognize that moustache anywhere. It was then he stepped back and gasped. He had to steady himself from fainting.

The man in the video was he. Himself.

He grasped for the edge of the desk to keep from falling. There, in the glass case, the gargoyle seemed to mock him, to chide him. The devil seemed to be laughing at him. At the fool he was.

Slowly, trembling, he opened the bottom drawer of his desk. He pulled it fully out of the wooden frame. There, in the bottom of the drawer were three bloody organs. Three hearts.

Just then he heard a knock on the front door. Outside three patrol cars of the police stood with their blue and red lights flickering. Staggering, he crept toward the front door. He unlocked it.

He had been caught. The nanny cam wasn't the only camera in the city it seemed.

÷

The auction for the Antique store would start in the morning. His relatives perused his collection, hoping to maybe get something of value for their own use before the auction began. His nephew stopped in front of the glass case.

He was enthralled by the carved marble demon inside. It spoke to him. Quickly, before anyone else could see, he wrapped the gargoyle in a linen tarp they had used to keep the dust off the antique furniture and whisked it to the trunk of his car.

It was museum quality, he could tell. He would make a fortune on it.

Symphonic Dissonance

Why was he here?

It was the question he kept repeating in his head. This was so totally outside his interest it hurt to even walk in the building. His girlfriend, Miki, had drug him here. She was the cause of his pain. She was the one who had insisted. Yes, it was Miki. Miki had been the one.

Ryan's girl, Miki, was a Music major. She was concentrating in vocals and the symphony was featuring a famous tenor today. Miki was so excited to see him; she had been a fan for a very long time. Ryan hadn't wanted to deprive her of the event, but why he had had to accompany her was a mystery. Probably because it was the job of the boyfriend to do so. Probably because it showed he cared. Probably, because it meant something to her.

They entered the lobby of the old theater. The wood carvings on the columns that held up the mezzanine level and the oil paintings that adorned the walls harkened back to a time long past. A time where limousines would pull up to the curb in front and spew their ladies and gentlemen onto the sidewalk. The men dressed in top hat and tails, the women in ermine and pearls.

Ryan would try and make the best of it. He put on his best fake smile as they walked past the ticket taker. It seemed they were in the third balcony. Three flights of stairs. They were the best seats Miki could afford on a student's salary. Ryan steeled himself for the climb. Why they couldn't take the elevator, he did not know.

"Uri?" A very old man with white hair approached. "Is that you?"

"Umm ..." Ryan had no idea who this nutbag was.

"Uri! It's been so long! What have you been up to?"

Ok, so this guy was getting insistent. Ryan turned to Miki to see if she knew the guy, but she had already left for their seats. He shook the man's hand and started to tell him that he must be mistaken. "I don't think you've ..."

"Carly, look who I've found!" The man was waving a group of his people over. "It's Uri!"

Carly approached and threw her arms out wide. "Uri! After so long!" She hugged Ryan like he was her long-lost son.

"Uri, I want you to meet our daughter, Kaitlin. Kaiti, this is *the* Uri Markovic, the toast of St. Petersburg!"

A young lady in full evening dress ambled over and shook Ryan's hand. "The violinist? The prodigy?" Kaitlin smiled and asked if she could take her picture by waving her phone at him and raising her eyebrows. Ryan nodded approval.

Now Ryan would have trouble picking out which one was the violin from choice between violin, viola and oboe. But the old man and his family seemed so excited and happy, he didn't want to harsh their mellow, so to speak. "Very nice to meet you all." He turned to go. Miki would be waiting.

"You must come and watch from our box!" The old man had grabbed his arm and began escorting him to the elevator.

Now Ryan didn't know if it was the prospect of using the elevator instead of the stairs, or if maybe Kaitlin was quite pretty. Or that he had never, ever seen anything from a private box, but Ryan decided to see where this could take him.

The family Ryan had taken up with were the Davenports, longtime supporters of the arts. They were avid patrons of all kinds of artistic expression, but their love would always center around the symphony and music. Being such large contributors to the enterprise, the symphony had dedicated their best box to their use. Ryan was a bit shocked when he beheld the opulence with which they would view the day's program.

The private box looked more like the lobby of a whore house to Ryan than something of culture. Everything was ensconced in heavy fabric or dark stained wood. There was even the hint of the smell of perfume.

At the back of the box lay an assortment of pastries and other snacks. A giant bottle of champagne was sitting in a silver bucket of ice. The waiter (or whatever they called him) asked if he would like a flute of the bubbling wine.

"Yes." That was all Ryan could muster right now. He was still quite awestruck at the grandeur of the room. The thick, handwoven carpeting. The velvet curtains. The gold that seemed everywhere. This was what he had been missing. He could get used to this.

They gave Ryan (or Uri as they knew him) the best seat at the front of the box. The chair was finished in gold leaf with a red velvet cushion for his bottom. The cushion felt nice on his buttocks, not like the metal benches they sat upon at the football games he frequented.

Ryan drank his champagne and as the warm glow that alcohol tends to produce waved over his body, Ryan started to understand why people like the symphony. He was having a great time.

Ryan squinted as he investigated the third balcony for his sweetheart. He couldn't make her out, the seats at the top were in shadow and too far away to really have any kind of resolution between body and body.

Kaitlin offered her opera glasses. "Try these."

"Thanks." Ryan put the glasses to his eyes and peered into the dark at the top of the richly ornate and gold-plated ceiling of the theater. There in the second to the last row, he found her, his Miki. She was intent on her program, ostensibly reading about the histories printed there. He felt a pang of guilt. She should be here, and he should be there.

"Who 's that you are searching?" Kaitlin was curious.

"Umm…" Now Ryan didn't want to blow his gig here by crushing the rather obvious interest young Kaitlin had in him, so his mouth produced the following without having engaged his brain very much. "My sister."

"Well, we should go get her and bring her here! Oh, Reynolds." Kaitlin waved to the waiter, or butler, or was it manservant? Anyway, Kaitlin waved Reynolds over. "See that someone brings Uri's sister here, won't you?"

"Yes, madame."

"She's … Uri where is she?"

Ryan was trapped. He had to keep going with the lie. "She's in the third balcony, she's the one with the blue dress and teal silk scarf. Here, look." Uri, no Ryan, gave the opera glasses to Reynolds and pointed.

"Yes, I see her sir. Right away." Reynolds left.

"You would think they would give someone as accomplished as you better seating?" Kaitlin frowned.

"It was a last-minute thing. They were the only seats left."

"Oh." Kaitlin was still visibly upset and looked like she was going to have a talk with someone when the concert ended.

The house lights of the theater began to dim.

The first violinist entered from stage left. He started to play a note on his violin and the rest of the orchestra echoed their instruments in an effort to get all of them in tune. Ryan liked this piece; it had a clean simplicity that appealed to him. What music! The sounds were thunderous.

When the tuning piece ended, a man entered from stage left. The crowd applauded. The guy must be famous, Ryan postulated. The man jumped on the little platform they had placed in the middle of the orchestra and began to wave a small magic wand at the musicians arrayed before him. The orchestra jumped to respond, and the real music started.

Ryan wasn't as fond of this piece of music. It had all kinds of intricacies that his untrained ear had trouble assimilating with his database of music knowledge. There were long stretches of low moaning strings followed by frenetic phrases from the brass and timpani. Ryan didn't know if it was the champagne or the music, but he began to nod off.

That is, until he felt a foot caressing his ankle. Kaitlin was been put in a saucy mood by the orchestra.

Ryan diplomatically moved his foot as if he hadn't noticed that he was invading Kaitlin's space. That made Kaitlin all the more aggressive. In time, though, the tenor, Placido Domenico, who they had all awaited, stepped onto the stage. The audience roared their pleasure.

Now if the orchestra had bored Ryan, the tenor singing opera in Italian did nothing to improve his interest. If it weren't for the insistent Kaitlin, he would have been shushed for snoring minutes after the great tenor began.

Ryan was about to make an excuse to leave when, after the piece the tenor performed, a young lady was introduced to the group.

"Miss Miki." Reynolds had found her.

"Oh, I'm am so glad they found you!" Kaitlin was the first to greet their new guest. "Your brother has been naughty in trying to keep you from us!"

The old man stood and shook Miki's hand. "I'm relieved that Uri's rather unfortunate features have not translated to his sister!" The old man winked the wink of a scoundrel and nudged Ryan, who had also risen, in the ribs.

Mrs. Davenport took Miki's arm. "Here. You must sit here."

Reynolds brought Miki a flute of champagne and topped off Ryan and Kaitlin's while he was at the job. Miki leered at her boyfriend. What the hell had he gotten them into! She leaned over to him.

"What the eff, Uri!" She let the word Uri play out in the long dulcet tones of the well-bred, or at least how they are parodied. "What in God's whole of creation are you doing!?" She said the words through clenched teeth.

The tenor began his second piece, so the group quieted down to listen respectfully. It had the same somnolent effect on Ryan as the first. Thankfully, Kaitlin had no diminution of her coquetry. Ryan would stay awake.

The third selection from the tenor was something more popular from Wagner. There were parts that Ryan could relate to. He thought he might have heard it in a Bug's Bunny cartoon. This selection, being the finale, was met with thunderous applause and a standing ovation by the audience.

The concert being over now, the Davenports huddled to give their reviews. Kaitlin was unsure of the woodwinds. They always seemed a little late to her. Mrs. Davenport thought the tenor was superb. No one argued with that assessment.

Miki huddled with her 'brother'. "What are you doing with that girl!? Is she who you want? Really?"

"She seems to be smitten with me. I just …"

"So that is what you want. Little Miss Prissy Davenport, huh?"

"That's not what I … "

"Fine. If that's they way you want it, two can play that game."

Old Mr. Davenport approached the pair. "We're having an afterparty backstage. We would be devastated if your two didn't attend."

Mrs. Davenport and Kaitlin chimed in as well. "Please do come. It will be so delightful. You can meet the maestro!?"

Miki was all in. She had long wanted to meet Placido Domenico. "We'd love to." She used her fake English accent for the words.

÷

Backstage, the entire company assembled around a few folding tables. The food wasn't as elegant as the private box, but there was plenty of booze. Ryan sampled the wine. It was domestic Californian. Not bad but not as good as the Imported stuff they had been drinking. Ryan powered through, though.

They had a bowl of gummy bears on the table. Ryan thought it peculiar to have a child's candy next to the wine, but he shrugged his shoulders and threw a couple into his mouth. He chewed the gummy goodness and washed it down with the wine.

Kaitlin cornered Ryan behind the stage curtain. "There you are, you naughty boy!" She threw herself at Ryan and kissed him.

"Umm … I … umm… well …" Ryan was surprised indeed.

Old Mr. Davenport was just retuning from the bathroom when he fell upon the two in an apparent lover's embrace. "Uri! My goodness, man! She's only seventeen years old!"

"She … what!? I never …" Ryan pushed the girl away.

"Come with me, Kaiti!" The old man was angry. He was serious. The girl followed him back to the party.

Ryan went back to the party as well. He had had enough of the symphony now. It was fun for a while, but the idea of being locked up for statutory rape or something didn't seem all that glamourous.

He looked for his girlfriend and maybe someday life partner. She was on the other side of the room flirting with the tenor. 'Hot stuff Mr. Domenico.' Ryan seethed the words under his breath. He visited the sparkling wine table.

Miki was having the time of her life. She was conversing with one of the giants in an industry that she aspired to join. The maestro virtuoso was giving her all kinds of career advice as well as flattering her into a girlish giggling fit.

"Oh, I could never do that!" Miki was sure she could in fact do that and do it rather well, but then again, she didn't want to sound conceited.

"You must come to Tuscany some time. You would only improve the beauty of the place." Domenico kissed Miki's hand.

Ryan wanted to puke. Such syrupy nonsense. Who did this guy think he was, chatting up his girl like that!? Ryan downed his glass of wine and approached the two, who were deeply involved in conversation.

"You poncy bitch wagon!" It was all his alcohol addled brain could spit out at the moment.

"Excuse me?"

Now poncy was maybe fair. The guy did have all of the affectations of a gad about town, a fop, a dandy, a toff. It was the bitch wagon that didn't make much sense. Was he going for a conveyance for female dogs, or maybe a vehicle devoted to the voicing of complaints? No one knew.

But what Ryan didn't know was that the gummy bears he had eaten were infused with the stuff of the marijuana plant. The psychotropic stuff. A single gummy bear was intended as a single dose. He had had maybe three or five. No one knew.

"I said you are a ponce and a bitch." Ryan tried to make some sense but failed at it. "Get your hands off of my wife!"

"Wife?" Placido turned to Miki who immediately dissuaded him of that notion. To have been flirting with him while married might be construed as tartish.

Ryan put up his hands to box. He would have this poncy fop if it was the last thing he would do. And as it turned out it was the last thing. At the symphony anyway.

Placido Domenico bopped him straight on the nose. The force of the blow caused blood to flow down Ryan's mouth and onto his shirt. The sound of the crack gave a cue that maybe something had broken inside. Miki and Kaitlin ran to Ryan.

"Are you hurt my darling?" That was Kaitlin.

"You stupid idiot." That was Miki.

÷

Later, in the emergency room, Miki smoothed the covers over her love, her life, her moronic boyfriend. The doctor had just finished taping up his broken nose and setting it so it would heal properly. He has eschewed the normal pain meds that would have been used in such a case. He didn't know what unwanted drug to drug interactions might occur between gummy bears, wine and pain meds.

Ryan was so out of it he consented to the procedure only to wince with pain at the procedure's execution. It would be hours before he would regain any kind of sanity. Miki would stay with him if only to be able to yell at him once he could understand what she was yelling about.

He turned to his beloved. "I love the symphony. When can we go again?" He tilted his head in memory of the good times they had had there.

Miki frowned. "No time soon. I think we may have been barred. Maybe for life."

"That's funny. Barrrrred. Haha." Ryan laughed but stopped when it hurt too much. "Barrrrrrrred..."

"Hilarious." Miki rolled up her magazine and tapped Ryan on the nose.

"Owwwww!"

Family Reunion

The sea was choppy that day. There were more than a couple of folks who leaned over the side and came back up with their hands to their mouths. The ferry was large enough to fit multiple passengers and their cargo, but not large enough to fully absorb the energy of the waves. The ferry carried on cutting a swath in the surface of a textured ocean. The ship persevered undaunted by the task.

Henry Boseman had made the journey on the ferry to meet for the first time his grandfather. The boy grew up in New York as the son of a mother who had fled the family in hopes of a life unfettered by greed and intrigue. She desired a life of caring and connection for her and her son.

He had waited long hours for the trip. Henry had been summoned by the lawyer of the family patriarch and hoped to reconnect with his roots. His grandfather had paid his passage to the family country retreat.

The young man rode on the ferry with ostensibly a group of businessmen in business suits. Their destination was the same as his, they sought the magnate, Reginald Thornton. Reginald had taken a small inheritance from his father and built a rather extensive empire in the buying and selling of other businesses. He was regarded (behind closed doors) as the king of the hostile takeover.

The boat pulled up to the dock and the captain yelled to the deckhand to jump out and tie her down. The drizzle made the wooden pier slippery, so the boy had trouble navigating it. The pier extended down to the great basalt towers that soared to define the cliffs above.

What ancient catastrophe had occurred to build this island lay as mystery to the group. The falling of night gave the cliff an otherworldly quality. The scene was one of eerie circumstance.

The passengers from the boat began their debarkation. There were carts arrayed by the dock house at the end of the dock for luggage. The passengers placed their bags here. They would be dragged up to the mansion above by the gardener, who waited patiently nearby. Henry eschewed placing his backpack there. He would carry it himself.

The climb to the top where the mansion lied, however, was the job for every person. There was no elevator, only a slender stairway carved in the side of the cliff by an unknown and unnamed people of yore.

Henry offered his arm to try and help one of the aging businessmen from the ferry manage the rain-soaked steps they must use, but the gentleman pushed him away maintaining that he could do it. He looked back at Henry. "Climb it like Everest, one foot in front of the other!" Henry followed the old codger, one step at a time. He kept a safe distance, but close enough to catch the old man should he falter.

Thornton, the owner of the mansion and their host, had chosen the Outer Hebrides for his summer house. The air was clean and crisp in summer without all the bother of heat and humidity that plagued the climes to the south. Here he could relax and enjoy the peace that came with isolation. Here, there was no one to bother him. There were no phones and no internet, save for a small office area. Thornton insisted on that.

The crew of the boat made ready to return to the mainland. They made this trip every other day, weather permitting, to bring the various foodstuffs and accoutrement that were needed to keep an island habitable. They were anxious to get back to their families and friends, now that the cargo had been safely transported. A storm was brewing to the northwest. They would make hast on the return not to get caught in its potentially hazardous grasp.

The passengers, huffing and puffing as they approached the great oaken door that granted access to the mansion, paused as they beheld the beauty of the house itself. The mansion boasted of 21 bedrooms, a solarium and a bowling alley. The residence occupied a large portion of the level ground of the island and had been built in the style of the ancient Scottish castles. The stone edifice was an imposing sight with its grand turrets and gargoyles posed to sit in protection of the manor.

The short businessman with noticeable girth stepped forward and, using the large brass knocker designed for such a task, alerted the staff inside of their arrival.

The giant oak door creaked open and a middle-aged man in formal attire greeted the party. This was ostensibly the butler.

"Won't you come inside."

The invitation was welcome to all as the slight drizzle had started to increase in intensity and the gentlemen were eager not to ruin their businessman hairdos. The short well-fed man pushed past the others and shook the butler's hand.

"Crowley, how good to see you again." He shook the butler's hand with such ferocity that the butler had to disengage the shake before it was completed. "It's been awhile, no?"

"Why yes. So good to see you as well." Crowley motioned with his right hand for him to enter the drawing room to the right.

Henry stepped forward and introduced himself to Crowley. "I'm Henry, Camelia's son. Mr. Thornton arranged my trip here."

"Oh yes. Mister Henry." Crowley extended his hand in a friendly shake. "I'm afraid there's bad news."

"Bad news?"

"Yes. Mr. Howard and his son, Carson won't be making the trip this weekend. It seems they have been called away."

Now Mr. Howard was his mother, Camelia's, brother and Carson was Henry's cousin. Henry had been looking forward to meeting them. "That's a shame."

"Of course, Mr. Thornton himself is here. He has planned some time with you tomorrow."

"That's good." Henry was a bit relieved he could relax a bit before meeting the great man.

The drawing room was furnished in a style congruent with the majesty of the mansion's façade. There were overstuffed chairs and a sitting divan. The coffee table was made of cherry wood with a marble inlay. There was wood paneling everywhere from the floor to the ceiling. The floor was covered with a plush garnet and gold carpeting. A great unlit fireplace adorned the room's end, the tile work exhibiting a Moroccan motif.

"Please enjoy an aperitif while we make your rooms ready." Crowley pointed to the array of liquor and cordials adorning the drinks cabinet by the stained-glass window.

Henry poured a cup of tea. He felt now might be a good time to meet the other guests. He approached the old man and introduced himself. "Hello, I am Henry Boseman, Camelia's son." He smiled.

"Hrrmmpphh." The old man returned to his drink without acknowledging the lad.

Henry was a bit put off by this obvious shun. The other men in suits didn't look any more friendly than the old man, so he decided to enjoy his beverage in peace by himself in the seat by the window.

The drawing room was furnished in an older style with overstuffed chairs and oil paintings adorning the wood paneled walls. There were two great windows in the room. The one where Henry was perched held a spectacular view of the grounds behind the mansion that one could not see from the sea approach.

The back housed a beautiful well-manicured garden with hedgerows and rose beds. Beyond the formal garden was a pasture and Henry could just make out a few white spots there. The spots were moving about. A closer look revealed the spots to be sheep. Henry marveled at the bucolic splendor of the scene as it stood in stark contrast to the stony sterility of the cliffs upon which the pastures were sitting.

The businessmen were getting louder and louder now in their administrations about this and that buyout or these and those labor unions. There was talk of EBIDA and pension obligations. There was ample fodder for lulling a young man to sleep, but Henry kept his wits about him. He whiled away the time trying to guess who the old people in the paintings might be.

The conversations in the room were interrupted by Crowley opening the doors to drawing room. "Gentlemen, your rooms are ready."

The group followed Crowley and the housekeeper to their rooms. Henry would refresh himself before dinner.

≠

Dinner was served in the great hall in the middle of the mansion. The ceiling soared above the oak table spanning the length of the hall. Great woven tapestries graced the stone walls of the cavernous room with two fireplaces warming the area from either end. The housekeeper and Crowley bid Henry to enter and be seated.

"Mr. Thornton regrets he will not be dining with you this evening." That was all the explanation Crowley would offer.

Henry took his seat at the head of the massive table. "Aren't any of the others joining me?"

"Food has been taken to the conference rooms for them."

The housekeeper brought over a silver tureen filled with a soup. Crowley ladled out a generous portion into Henry's bowl in the place setting in front of him.

Henry regarded the concoction swimming in his soup bowl. The broth looked familiar but there were some rather alien bits floating about. "What kind of soup is it then?"

"The cook's specialty. Coquille and tripe."

Henry had no idea what a coquille was, but he didn't like the sound of that tripe thing. He decided to take a taste anyway and to his surprise the soup was remarkably delicious. He finished the entire serving.

The main course was something much more recognizable, roasted lamb and vegetables. Henry's dinner ended with a preparation called 'Sticky Toffee Pudding'. Crowley poured heavy cream on the dessert. One spoonful of the heavenly sweet and Henry would be forever a Sticky Toffee Pudding fan.

Crowley recommended a glass of cognac in the solarium as an after-dinner enjoyment. The combination sounded good to Henry and so he took his snifter of the aged distillate of alcohol and headed for the solarium.

What awaited him in the solarium was a verdant garden of plants from all over the world. 'The gardener here is a bit of a genius.' Henry whispered the words as his eyes took in with amazement the symphony of horticulture that they beheld.

Henry took a seat by the giant windows that fed the solarium its sunlight. He watched as the coming storm advanced over the sea beyond, its lightning punctuating its movements in a display of unbridled violence.

The savagery of the storm outside lay in contrast to the melodious opera that the two canaries in the banyan tree behind him were warbling. The combined effect of this overload to his senses and the alcohol from the cognac produced a rather profound peace in his soul. Henry was content. He wanted for nothing.

Except maybe sleep. He was quite jetlagged.

$$\neq$$

The morning dawned and Henry popped down to the kitchen for some coffee. The cook was busy prepping some kind of dish over a steaming pot n the stove. Henry spied the coffee pot in the corner and helped himself.

"Some eggs with that coffee?" The cook took a break from stirring the pot to ask.

"Just coffee, thanks."

"Some toast then"

"No, I'm fine. Thanks."

Henry sipped the black liquid and contemplated his day. Today was the day he would meet his grandfather. After all this time not knowing he even existed it would be a major event in his life. He sipped some more coffee.

Crowley entered the kitchen carrying a bunch of flowers. "Lots blooming even now." He left the blooms on the kitchen counter ostensibly for the housekeeper to arrange in the house. "Oh, Mr. Henry! Almost missed you there."

"Good morning!" Henry toasted the butler with his cup. "Today's the day!"

Crowley folded his hands and approached Henry. With bowed head and lowered tones Crowley gave Henry the bad news. "I'm afraid Mr. Thornton isn't going to be able to see you today." Crowley looked skyward. "He's got a bit of a crunch going on with the other guests, I'm afraid."

Henry was crestfallen. He slumped on the stool upon which he was perched. "Well, I guess there's always tomorrow." Henry smiled a halfhearted smile.

"Indeed. Indeed." Crowley left the kitchen for other destinations in the mansion.

Henry was not about to waste the day. Having returned to his room and fetching his backpack, he set out for the gardens and beyond. He wanted to explore this magnificent island that housed them. He checked his pack for his art supplies.

"You'll want a slicker." The cook picked up a grey raincoat from the hooks by the door and tossed it to Henry. "We don't know what the weather will be, but we do know there'll be rain."

Henry donned the frock and exited the massive stone structure into the formal gardens. The designer of the garden had laid it out in a structured pattern that spoke more of geometry than botany. The hedges were closely cropped and the walkways pristine of weeds. Henry's walk in the garden was one of quiet meditation as he appreciated the work that been put forth to exact such order out of the chaos of nature.

Reaching the end of the garden, Henry ventured forth to the more wild and untamed parts of the island. Here wildflowers bloomed amid a sea of grasses. There were very few trees but quite a few bushes. The sheep had free rein, they wandered about as they wished.

Henry walked to the edge of the cliff and looked down to the pounding surf below. The sea was still rough from the storm of the night before and the waves crashed high when they hit the immoveable rock of the island. Henry was tempted to sketch here, but something caught his fancy out of the edge of his vision.

Henry followed the cliff's edge to a place that was filled with little birds flying in and out over the cliff and into the sea and back. Creeping closer and closer the birds appeared to be part waterfowl, part parrot. They had orange webbed feet and the body of a duck, but the rounded orange beak much like a parrot. In between was a coat of black feathers on the back and white on the belly. The head of the beast had two flattened areas on each side of the head. These areas were covered in white with a black eye in the middle. Henry had never seen anything like these birds, and they began to fascinate him.

Henry positioned himself near the rim of the cliff with his sketch pad in hand. The little birds would fly up from the sea (probably fishing he suspected?) and then proceed to waddle past him into their small nests they had hollowed in grassy ground. The little buggers didn't seem to notice Henry, or if they did, they were not concerned.

Henry sketched the birds using the sea beyond to mark the scale in the composition. His fingers flew as pencils came out from the backpack and scratched the off-white paper on his sketch pad. Finally satisfied with the drawing, Henry pulled a tin of watercolor paint and a brush from the pack.

Looking around for water, a light drizzle began to fall. 'Perfect timing.' Henry whispered his good luck. He collected the water in the lid of the tin box and began forming great swatches of color across his sketch of the birds. In time he was satisfied. The work was completed.

He was just putting away his art supplies when he heard a great whooshing sound coming from the sea. Out in the Atlantic Ocean a small dot appeared that began to grow in size. The noise grew in volume.

The noisy dot turned out to be a helicopter that landed on the other side of the mansion from where he was drawing the birds. Henry decided the rain was heavy enough he would go back inside for the day and so he headed back the way he came.

Before he reached the house, the helicopter took off again and vanished from sight. It must have been something important, Henry postulated. His understanding was that most folks came to the mansion by the ferry.

$$\neq$$

Dinner that night came with more bad news.

"I'm afraid Mr. Thornton has been called away." Crowley tried to break the news slowly. "It will be quite some time before he returns."

"Oh, that must have been why the helicopter…" Henry was putting the pieces together.

"Indeed, yes." Crowley offered Henry some caviar.

"Not sure who the first one was to eat a fish egg, but he must have been brave!" Henry tried another halfhearted smile.

Henry ate his dinner in silence. He was beginning to see why his mother might have left for New York. He would have to return home, without meeting anyone. "I guess I'll have to take the ferry back then." He turned to Crowley with inquisitive eyes.

"I'll radio them. They can be here in the morning."

$$\neq$$

The boat arrived and Henry gathered up his belongings for the trip home. He stopped by the front door as Crowley was busy fluffing up the flower arrangement on the table in the middle of the foyer.

Henry unzipped his backpack. "Here. Will you give this to my grandfather?" Henry tore the painting of the birds out of the sketch pad.

"Why, it's quite good. You have a brave hand with the brush." Crowley held the painting up to the light to get a better look.

"It may just be his only chance of ever seeing them." Henry referenced the birds there. He zipped his backpack and headed out and down the stone staircase to the dock.

"Take care, Mr. Henry!"

The boat was already loaded when he arrived. Two businessmen were seated. Henry guessed that they hadn't been important enough to make the helicopter. The one sitting behind the luggage looked like a puker for sure.

Henry decided to sit on the front. Upwind.

Miss Prog Nosis

By Winston Roberts and Stephen Kanney

The diagnosis had been given. It was rough. She didn't know how she was going to tell him. It was devastating news that must be handled with the utmost delicacy. It would hurt him. It always hurt the ones that loved the most. She poured a cup of tea and waited for him to return home from working. Just a few more minutes to formulate her speech. Just minutes before his life would be forever changed.

Silvia Collins lived in an old craftsman bungalow with her husband, Noah. Silvia had been feeling pain in her stomach area for weeks and had gone to the doctor to see if there might be a remedy. She met all the appointments her doctor recommended, and the tests had come back. Silvia had stage 4 pancreatic cancer.

Pancreatic cancer was one of the bad ones. The survival rates were not good for the disease. Her doctor had told her she might have four months left, if that. Silvia was afraid of dying, that was sure. But the fear that was more immediate was the telling of the diagnosis to her husband.

Silvia raised the hot brown floral liquid to her mouth. All she had in the cupboard was Earl Grey. She loathed the bergamot flavor in the tea, but hard times call for hard measures. She swallowed the brew, the scent of old lady's perfume filling her nasal passages.

Just then, she heard Noah pulling up the driveway into the garage. The moment was at hand. She steeled herself. She had to be strong and not let down. He would need her strength now; she must endeavor even more because her own strength was waning.

"I'm home!" Noah threw his keys in the bowl by the back door.

"In here." Silvia called back to her mate. Her voice cracking as she said the words. She would have to do better.

"How did it go at the doctor?" Noah had been worrying.

"Not good. You should sit."

Silvia laid out the bitter news as best she could. She related what the doctor had said about the cancer and the statistics about survivability. She wanted to break down and wail as her husband did when the realization that she was in the last phase of her life hit him. It hit hard. She hugged her man and together they sat in the kitchen sobbing and shivering with the grief.

"First Mom, and now you." Noah finally regained a modicum of composure. "It's not fair." Noah's mother had died not yet two years ago of breast cancer.

"I know sweetheart." She rubbed Noah's back. "If I could I would stay with you forever, you know that, right?"

"I know." Noah kissed his wife even with the mucous flowing on his face.

Nothing much more was said. Nothing much more could be said, or in actuality nothing much more needed to be said. The couple ate their dinner in silence and went early to bed. It would be a fitful night. Neither slept much. The worry and anxiety would not allow it. They tossed and got up and laid down until morning.

The days passed. Silvia began the process of deciding just what exactly she would do with the four months she had been given. She decided not to tell friends. She didn't want to ruin her last days with all the 'How are you doing?' questions. What she wanted was one last vacation. One last time alone with her Noah.

Noah booked the vacation. They would spend a week in the Caribbean. They had honeymooned there. They had spent a wonderful time there and would relive that one last time.

Noah had seen his Mother suffering under the last stages of her cancer. The chemotherapies. The pain. Noah did not want that for his beloved. No, he could not and would not bear that again. He had a plan for that. A plan that he could implement after the vacation. He would wait until then. He must wait until then.

It was a Tuesday, after they returned that Noah put his plan in action. Silvia has left for her first consultation with the specialist. He had the whole morning to work. He visited the medicine cabinet.

Inside the cabinet he found her pain medication. The doctor had prescribed the pain meds. There didn't seem to be much worry in giving her the maximum strength. She would die before she would become addicted to the opioids contained in the bottle.

The instructions on the bottle read, 'Take one every six hours as needed, not to exceed 4 a day.' He took eight pills from the bottle and put them in his shirt pocket.

A visit to the kitchen later and he found the container of tea bags that she used. He would throw them all away save one. He gingerly opened the last tea bag and separated the gauze at the top removing the staple that held the string. He pulled the eight pills from his shirt pocket and opened each capsule and let their tiny white nuggets of pain medicine fill the top of the tea bag.

Carefully, he folded the gauze back over and reattached the staple, using a butter knife to fold the metal tines of the staple back over to seal the bag. He picked up the tea bag and held it to the light. If he looked closely enough, he could see the tiny white powder nubs in the bag. He hoped his beloved would not look so closely.

Replacing the tea bag in the cardboard container, he put it back in its place on the kitchen shelf. He closed the door and made his way to the garage. He would spend the day at his office. It would be the perfect alibi. No one would question a lady with only four months to live, first of all dying let alone, secondly committing suicide. He was doing this for her. He could not bear the thought of her suffering in her last days like his mother had done. He would not let that be her fate. He would not. He dared not.

The workday over, Noah said goodbye to some co-workers. It would reinforce his alibi. They would remember him saying goodbye. He got in his car and headed home. Home to his wife, now asleep forever. Her fight with life was over. She could rest in peace now.

Noah pulled the car into the garage like he had done so many times before. He opened the back door and threw his keys into the bowl. He crept to the kitchen. Had Silvia brewed her usual end of day tea? He turned the corner to find his wife sitting in her chair at the kitchen table. She was awake and alert. A part of Noah's spirit leapt in joy at the sight. He could have yet another day with his love.

"Good you're home!" Silvia jumped to her feet and hugged her man. "Good news! I'm cancer free!"

"What!?" Noah pushed her away and looked at her straight in the eyes. Was she somehow lying? Could this be true?

"They mixed up the tests. They gave my doctor the results for some other poor lady."

"What!?" The horror of the circumstance Noah found himself confronting was blinding. What if she had brewed the tea? What if ... The possibilities were too horrific to consider.

Noah's legs began to buckle. He reached for the back of a kitchen chair.

"Here honey. Sit down." Silvia helped him right himself in the chair.

"Here. I made some tea. Drink."

Noah took the cup. He considered what he must do. He deserved to drink the brew. He was guilty of attempted murder. Drinking would only be fair justice.

Noah took the cup by its handle. He threw it against the wall.

"Why tea, when we should have champagne!?"

Noah picked up his sweetheart and carried out of the house. They needed to celebrate.

The Forty Percent Genius

He hung up the phone with his wife. She had been elated at the news. He would be awarded the Copley Medal for his research in CRISPR-Cas9 and its implications for neurodegenerative disease. There was even talk of a Nobel. The recognition had come after decades of work and it would be the culmination of a lifetime of sacrifice by them both.

She had asked him to pick up a bottle of champagne on his way home. They would celebrate. He boarded the bus that he took every day to and from the lab. The familiar smells of sweat and urine permeated the bus. He got a seat near the front. That was almost never empty.

The bus was headed for the liquor store in the strip mall down the street from his home. He had never liked driving. The bus driver knew the streets and the traffic laws. He would rely on that. His stop loomed in the front window of the bus. He pulled the cord, indicating his wish to disembark.

At the liquor store he headed for the wine section. Not knowing which wines were champagne and which were not, he asked the gentleman stacking bottles for some help.

"Hi. I need a bottle of champagne."

The young man placed the last bottle on the shelf and looked at the aging scientist. "Do you want sparkling wine, or the real thing?"

"Umm …" The winner of the Copley Medal stroked his ample graying beard. "She said champagne."

"Well there are several very good sparkling wines that don't come with the price tag of champagne. We have some excellent California varietals."

"Umm …" The older man was lost. "How about that one?" He pointed to a bottle with a pony on the label.

"Actually, that's a Pinot. It's a decent wine but doesn't have the bubbles you might desire…"

"OK, can you just pick one?"

The young man stood back and scanned his inventory. He reached up and pulled a large bulbous bottle from the shelf. "Here. This one is quite tasty and it's not too expensive."

The scientist expressed his gratitude and headed for the register to pay. The woman from behind the counter was looking at her phone. He had to get her attention. He coughed.

"Just one bottle?" The young lady snapped her bubble gum as she started to ring up the order.

"Yes."

"That'll be $19.85."

The gentleman rummaged through his raincoat and pants looking for his wallet. He finally happened upon it in the inside pocket of the raincoat. He opened the leather money container and leafed through the expired coupons and bits of paper layered inside the pouch to find his credit card. He placed the card in the side slot of the credit card reader and swiped.

"That's a chip card." The woman seemed exasperated at the man's seeming incompetence. "You have to insert it in the bottom slot."

The older man placed his credit card in the bottom slot. The lady sighed the sigh of one completely unhappy with their job.

"The other way." When he had trouble she offered, "The other, other way."

The chip card finally engaged properly the computers whizzed and buzzed to exchange some of his money at his bank into the bank that the liquor store used to store their cash. The machine started to beep. The older scientist looked confused.

"You can remove it now." The young woman rolled her eyes.

Grabbing his wine and his credit card, the scientist walked the rest of the way home. He was still beaming from the exciting news about the Copley. He could not wait to share the moment with his wife. She had been his constant support over the years, and they needed to commemorate this achievement. It had been won with a lot of sweat and surrender of the more frivolous things of life.

The older man fumbled with his keys as he approached the front door of his home. Finding the brass key that fit the lock of his house, he pushed and turned. The front door locked at the turning. He grabbed the knob and turned. The door wouldn't open, it was locked, of course.

Looking confused again, he tried his key again. This time he turned the key in the opposite direction. Success! Opening the front door, he heard his wife calling from the kitchen. "Dinner's almost ready!"

He made his way to the back of the house and pulled forth his bottle from its brown paper bag that the liquor store had provided. "I got the champagne."

"Oh good! Why don't you open it; I'll get the lamb on the table."

He ventured into the dining room and opened the top drawer of the china cabinet where they kept the corkscrew. He put the sharp end of the screw on top of the bottle of sparkling wine and began the twisting motion that would have been important in removing a cork. This bottle, however, had one of those plastic tops that you must remove by hand. The corkscrew was not needed.

Onward he endeavored. The screw was penetrating the plastic top all right, but when he tried to pull the 'cork' out of the bottle the screw came out empty. All that remained to attest to the procedure recently completed was a hole in the plastic top.

He looked at the bottle. An idea presented itself. He took the bottle down to the workbench in the basement. He levered the bottle between two cardboard boxes of various and sundry and using a hammer began to lightly ping the top of the bottle. His aim was to loosen the top to make it easier to remove.

He pinged once too many times and the top of the bottle cracked and exploded as the pressure inside the bottle was great. It had been made greater by the pinging of the hammer. The bottle produced a fountain of bubbles that shot high in the air. When the shower of wine was completed, all he had left was a broken bottle half full of wine.

Another idea hatched in that magnificent brain of his and he visited the kitchen to implement the project. He searched the cabinets for a large measuring cup that had a lip for pouring and a rusty metal strainer.

"What'cha doin' there?" His wife was curious at his choice of kitchenware.

"Just opening the wine."

Back in the basement again, he poured what was left of the wine from the bottle through the strainer and into the measuring cup. What had begun as light-yellow wine of excellent quality was now a slightly orange liquid, having been tainted by the rust in the strainer.

He returned to the dining room to find his wife just finishing setting the table with her fine china and silver. A carving platter lay in the middle of the table beside the lighted candles. A perfectly roasted leg of lamb rested in the middle of the platter with assorted roasted root vegetables adorning the ring of the carving board.

He put the two glasses he had procured from the kitchen on the table. They were the glasses his kids had used in their youth. He set the one with Wilma Flintstone in front of his wife's place setting. Barney Rubble was placed by his. He poured the wine.

His wife raised her glass for a toast. "To your recent success and the successes to come. May your best days be in front of you!"

He picked up his glass and raised it to his lips. But before tasting, he responded. "None of this would have been possible without you, dear."

They drank. She quickly placed her beverage back on the table. He squinted and held the glass to the light. It tasted somewhat livery. 'Oh well.' What did he know about wine anyway?

She decided to start the small talk. "I heard on the radio that people are spending almost forty percent of their working lives at work. It's up from thirty-six just ten years ago."

"Hmmm … That seems low to me."

"It does somehow. I guess they must include sleep time there?"

"Who has time to sleep?" They both laughed.

He carved and they ate. He drained the last of his wine and poured another draught. "Some more for you?" He raised his eyebrows as he tempted his bride with another glass of the bubbly.

She put her hand over her glass. "None for me, thanks." She went back to eating. Eventually she gave the excuse. "I still have work to do later."

He nodded in agreement. "I have a grant application to go over myself."

The meal over, he offered to help clean up. "Let me wash those honey."

She immediately grabbed the dishes he was trying to pick up. "No dear! I will do it."

He went to his study. She breathed a sigh of relief. Those were her mother's dishes.

The Whispers

A lone old man, his wife having passed, and his kids moved away, toddled onto the front porch of his house and lay his breakfast on the table beside his chair. He zipped his jacket closed; the air was nippy. Sitting down, he raised his cup and drank. The memories of a life of pain and woe filled his thoughts.

The wind whisked through the limbs of the trees just starting their annual denudation. The gentle breeze caught the branches and made them dance in the ballet of ancient origin. The wind breathed,

'Why do we love? Why do we live?'

The sun, low in the sky, put forth its radiance, blinding the observer. It shouted in soft tones,

'Look away in shame.'

The cold embraced all that dared venture forth from hearth and home. It gave no mercy. It took what it wanted. The cold evinced its truth,

'Kiss me and die.'

The black birds on the telephone wire cackled their daily song.

'We know what you did.'

In time, clouds blew in and covered the raging sun. Slowly at first, then with resolve, the clouds gave up their moisture to let it fall softly to the ground. The drizzle coated everything it touched in a silvery mirror of precipitation.

The old man raised his cup to his lips and sipped the hot black brew once more. He welcomed the lift the coffee would provide. The warmth was just a bonus. The liquid passed his lips and oozed down to his stomach, bathing it in its warmth.

Something was stirring in the front yard. There, under the pile of leaves. He stepped from the porch to investigate. Gingerly, he rustled the pile, hoping to expose what was contained underneath. He stood in surprise. The leaves housed a baby rabbit.

The little bugger was shivering from the wet and the cold. Its mother was nowhere to be seen. The little brown guy was skinny, emaciated. He picked up the rodent and carried it softly in his hands to his perch on the porch.

He nestled the still quivering rabbit in his jacket, providing it with his body warmth. The table beside his chair held a plate with a small piece of uneaten toast on it. He offered the bread to the little bundle of fur. The rabbit ate.

The baby rabbit slept, firmly ensconced in his jacket. He could feel its little heart beating. He felt the rise and fall of its tiny chest as it breathed.

The slumber of his visitor was infectious. In time, the old man would succumb to its wiles and fall into a deep sleep. His rest was fitful, filled with the nightmares of his life of woe.

$$\neq$$

One year later, the old man, once again, performed his morning ritual. He brought his breakfast to the front porch. He nestled into his favorite chair and observed the world passing by.

An adult rabbit, Hippity Pippity as she had been named, followed the old man to the porch followed by four little baby rabbits. The brood of rodents played at the old man's feet. The old man picked up the smallest of the babies and rubbed its head as it rested on his lap.

The old man sipped his coffee. The black birds on the telephone wire cackled their daily song.

'Good morning!'

The baby rabbit on his lap became impatient. It wanted to play with its littermates. He gently placed the bundle of fur and ears on the porch floor. The sun beamed bright on the horizon.

'What a day to be alive!'

The old man leaned back in his chair. He closed his eyes to reflect. The wind whistled and wheezed its message as it ruffled the browning leaves of the trees.

'We live to love.'

A Birthday Surprise

His wife was busy dusting and vacuuming. She never dusted and vacuumed. Not this early in the morning. Not ever. He knew what was going on. He was on to her. She was plotting something. Something like maybe a birthday party? Maybe his birthday party? It was his birthday day after all.

He decided he better shower and shave and look presentable as there was likely to be all kinds of well-wishers and hanger-on's that would be filling the house later. He wanted to look good for his adoring fans. So, up the stairs he climbed to the bedroom to clean and clothe. He needed to keep up his rep as a fashion icon. He laughed as he imagined that. His aging, somewhat rotund physique was not what the fashion industry valued.

Back downstairs he approached his wife. She was setting the dining room table with four place settings and accompanying silverware. It was to be an intimate birthday luncheon.

"What's up?" He winked at her as he said the words.

"Oh, nothing…" She smiled. "Just tidying up…"

He smiled as well. He decided to plop himself in front of the TV for some football action therapy while he waited. She would spring the 'surprise' on him when she was ready.

The game was slow with all the penalties and neither offence was moving the ball much. And so, the hypnotic drone of the TV lulled him into a light slumber. His mind drifted to the absurdities of the dream world.

He was abruptly awakened by the ringing of the front doorbell. He pulled the lever on his recliner chair and sat upright. He rubbed his eyes, not really knowing where or even who he was.

"Happy Birthday, buddy!" It was his brother Carl.

"Happy Birthday!" His sister-in-law, Maddie, gave him a one-armed hug, she had a cake carrier on the other arm.

He stretched and yawned. "Thanks!"

His wife, Laura, had followed his relatives into the TV room. "Let me take that for you." She grabbed Maddie's cake carrier. "Looks delicious!"

"Lemon Lime pie." Maddie beamed with pride. "It's Dan's favorite!"

He, Dan, recoiled in horror. The words chilled him to the bone, 'Lemon Lime pie'. I hadn't been but three or four years ago when Maddie had made him that same exact pie for his birthday. It was a no-bake pie that included some eggs. Maddie and Carl maintained a condo in town to use when they saw their kids but came back to town rather infrequently.

Maddie had used eggs that had sat in her refrigerator at the condo for over 6 months on that pie. He held back a bit a vomit at the thought. The pie had given him the worst case of food poisoning he had ever experienced. And now, Maddie and the pie had returned for another round of pain.

There had been hours of vomiting and diarrhea before. There had been body aches and headaches. He had prayed for release from the poisoning back then. At his lowest he had prayed for the sweet release of death. His stomach rebelled at the sight of the cake carrier now. He had to repress a second wave of nausea.

Dan had never told Maddie of the illness. Maddie was a sweet woman of intense kindness and fragility. Knowing that she had poisoned him would have caused her grief. She would have stewed in an empathetic pit of despair had he alerted her to the problem. He was the best man at her wedding for goodness sake.

He had remained silent. He would pay for that silence, now, it seemed.

The lunch progressed with much of the same old chit chat in which most families and friends engage. It wasn't long before they were all caught up on the goings on since their last meeting.

Laura had prepared some of Dan's favorites. Fried Chicken with roasted potatoes and asparagus. Dan wasn't a complicated man; he knew what he liked to eat. Dessert was looming, however. Dan was getting nervous about the dessert.

Laura cleared the plates away and she and Maddie disappeared into the kitchen area in low whispers. Everyone knew what was coming next. But not everyone knew the import of what came next. That was the purview of Dan alone.

"Happy Birthday to you ..." Maddie and Laura started the song.

Carl chimed in. "Happy Birthday to you ..."

Before the final 'Happy Birthday' was sung, Dan steeled himself for what was next.

"OK who wants how big a slice!?" Maddie was behind the pie with a large knife and a pie spatula.

"None for me, thanks. I'm on a diet." Laura was always on a diet.

"I've got a colonoscopy tomorrow and can't". Carl hadn't even partaken of the chicken, so he was excused of course.

"Well I'm doing a cleanse, so I can't partake. How about a nice big slice for the Birthday Boy!?" Maddie drove the knife deep into the pie and cut a rather large wedge.

"No, smaller!" Dan begged with his eyes as well as his words. "That's too much!" Dan was considering his own cleanse that would begin in about eight hours.

Maddie acceded and cut a smaller, if not still large slab of the citrusy dessert.

The three watched as Dan picked up his fork and gingerly played with the pie. Dan thought that if they would just stop looking, he might be able to hide some of the pie in his napkin, or on the floor. He was looking for a way out. Any way out.

It was not to be. The trio looked on to gain the enjoyment of watching their loved one eat his favorite pie on his day of days for the year.

Dan took a forkful of pie and ate.

The three smiled.

Dan ate another. Then another. Then a painful one more. Then, in an act of surrender, Dan finished his pie.

Maddie looked to his eyes to tell if he had enjoyed it. Dan met her gaze and realized what was required of him.

"Ummm …" Dan would have normally remarked, 'Ummm … good.', but couldn't get the word 'good' out of his mouth. His body refused to form the word. His body knew what was coming.

Maddie and Carl said their goodbyes and Dan waited for the eight hours to see if he would live or die.

Eight hours later found Dan kneeling in worship before the porcelain gods of the master bathroom. His only words to his wife would be, "Put that pie down the disposal!"

He would think on the events of the day and congratulate himself that he had asked for a smaller slice. He gauged he may not have made it, had the slice been larger.

$$\neq$$

A year passed and Dan got an email from his brother that they would be heading back to town. It being near his birthday again, and the events of the last birthday firmly etched in his mind, Dan was desperate. He lay back in his desk chair to contemplate the eating of yet another ptomaine infused Lemon Lime pie.

A thought occurred to Dan. It wasn't that long ago, a couple of years maybe. Carl had given him a key to the condo should there ever be any kind of emergency or etc. Where had he put that key? He was sure he put it somewhere where it would be safe. Right now, it was very safe as he didn't know where it even was.

Dan rifled through his desk drawer. No luck, except he did find that USB drive he had been looking for last week. His next idea was the kitchen pantry. They seemed to put all their keys there. It made them accessible to the entire family.

In the pantry he found the extra car keys. The key to the shed. A key to a job he had left three years ago. He was about to give up when he noticed a small rectangular box situated under some cookbooks in the corner. Dan remembered. The key was put there.

Now for the plan. He would go over after dinner and remove the offending poisonous eggs from the condo. Maddie would have to buy fresh eggs. Voila! The perfect plan.

He told Laura of his plan to steal the chicken embryos from Maddie. Laura rolled her eyes.

"Just tell already. She can take it!"

Dan couldn't bear the thought of intentionally hurting his sister-in-law. She had always been so kind to him. Carl was more like a father to him that an older brother. He would break into their condo instead in the dark of night and steal items from their refrigerator. That seemed better to Dan.

Night fell and Dan drove over to the condo. He put the key in the door lock and almost effortlessly gained entry into the two-bedroom, one bath apartment. He tiptoed to the kitchenette. Why he tiptoed he did not know, but less noise seemed prudent in some way.

The door of the refrigerator had a shelf with those indentations for the eggs. Maddie had not used that. Dan looked deeper into the cooler. There were boxes of juice and a bottle of wine. A six-pack of cola blocked the view of something behind. Dan move the cola and there they were. The box of eggs. He picked up the carton and closed the refrigerator door.

"It's you!" Dan stood face to face with a Carl wielding a baseball bat.

"It's me, Dan!" Dan stated the obvious.

"You scared the dickens out of me!" Carl put down the bat and grabbed at his heart, ostensibly to calm it down, to reduce the rate of beating.

Maddie slowly entered the apartment, looking around the corner of the door first.

"It's only Dan. Come on in." Carl motioned for her to enter. It was safe.

"What'cha got there?" Maddie pointed to the eggs in Dan's hands.

"Ummm …" Dan was caught and had not a good alibi ready. "Eggs?"

"Why are you taking our eggs?" Maddie was confused. They sold eggs at every grocery.

"Ummm …" Dan stalled for time to think of why he would have to come to their condo for eggs. "Laura needs them." That's it. Blame Laura.

"Oh." Maddie was satisfied. "But leave me two of them OK? I'm planning on a surprise for your birthday!"

Dan turned green. He opened the carton and gave Maddie two of the eggs. His stomach groaned.

"OK, see you guys soon then"

"Of course, we'll be at your BBQ." Maddie smiled a wry smile.

$$\neq$$

Dan's birthday arrived and with it, Carl and Maddie. Laura invited the neighbors as well. Laura made the event a back-yard barbeque this year. Dan reveled in the well wishes of family and friends. He slapped backs and drank one or two too many beers.

The dinner portion over the dessert would be presented. Dan was dreading the dessert. He took a massive gulp of his beer, hoping the alcohol might in some way counterbalance the poison in the pie. He looked helplessly to the gatherers for help, but all he could evince was a group of friends and family with silly grins. And then, Maddie's cake carrier was brought forth from the kitchen and placed on the table in front of Dan.

Dan's stomach immediately reacted. A bit of sudsy beer and BBQ chicken regurgitated into Dan's throat. He sat motionless as Maddie removed the top from the carrier. He would say nothing. He could say nothing. Lemon Lime pie was to be his downfall, he knew it. It would be how he would die, how he would meet his maker.

"Voila!" Maddie revealed her creation for all to see.

There, before Dan, was a beautiful cherry pie. A cherry pie that doesn't require a single egg. The crust of the pie had been browned by the high heat of an oven and the cherry filling that had bubbled out between the lattice structure of crust on the top had been caramelized to a point where there was a crusty gooey surface to the top. There was no way that any bacterium could survive such heat.

"I decided to go cherry this year." Maddie smiled at her brother-in-law.

The gang started in on the birthday song. Dan couldn't help but smile. There would be no Lemon Lime pie this year. He could eat the cherry pie with impunity. Nothing could survive the heat of an oven.

When the song was over, Dan proclaimed in a loud voice.

"Cut me an extra-large slice!" Dan dive into the pie with such gusto that the crowd began to murmur at the bestial nature of his consumption of the sugary dessert.

Dan would not pass up his chance. He must put a thought in Maddie's brain. He spoke, impolitely maybe, with his mouth full of pie and a huge grin on his face.

"I fink cherry iz my new faborit!"

LOST IN FRENETIC CATATONIA

Made in the USA
Lexington, KY
09 November 2019